TWENTY-FIVE MEMORIES OF VIGGO MACDUFF

KATE GORDON

ODYSSEY
BOOKS

Published by Odyssey Books in 2017

www.odysseybooks.com.au

A Cataloguing-in-Publication entry is available from the National Library of Australia

ISBN: 978-1-925652-29-1 (pbk)

ISBN: 978-1-925652-30-7 (ebook)

Cover photo and design by Michelle Lovi

ONE

I wipe the chocolate from my chin with the back of my hand.

That's it. The last. Number twenty-five.

I look down at the glitter on my fingers. They stroke the tattered remains of what was once a reindeer and Santa. Now it's ripped and torn, and bears little resemblance to the happy whole it was before.

A bit like my heart.

I groan, my forehead dropping to my shimmering palms. Did I just think that?

Beezus is curled at my feet. He's gazing up at me disparagingly, as if he read my mind.

"Yes," I groan. "I did just compare my heart to a used-up advent calendar. Kill me now."

Beezus smiles, his little ferret fangs pushing against his bottom lip.

"I know," I say, picking him up and plonking him on my lap. I scratch him behind the ears and he purrs. "I'm being a loser. But you don't get it, Bee. You've never been in love. You've never had your heart ripped to shreds. You've never—"

Beezus gives a little start as my phone begins to ring. I wince. I'm going to have to change my ringtone.

Nobody this heartbroken should be allowed to listen to "The Luckiest". Even the first few bars. Even knowing that Ben Folds is no longer married to the lady he wrote that song for.

I look down at the flashing screen. It's Emily.

I tap the red hang up icon. I feel horrible and guilty. But I can't handle talking to anybody right now, except Beezus.

"I'm sorry it's not been a better Christmas. It's my fault. I ruined everything. I just couldn't—"

Rap Rap Rap!

It's my turn to jump. The loud noise came from my bedroom window. "Who's that?" I whisper to Beezus. Emily is in Noosa for the holidays. And my entire family went without me to Debbie's house in Launceston. Which means it has to be …

"Be vewwy quiet, Bee," I whisper, "and he might just go a—"

"Connie Chase, I know you're up there. I can see your Vans!"

"Damn," I grumble. "Betrayed by skate shoes. Could today get any worse?"

"Connie? Come on. It's me. Your supposed best friend."

I peek over the windowsill. "Not in the mood for a lecture, Jeremiah," I call down. "So you can just go back to listening to your new Opeth CD, or whatever metalhead thing it was that you were doing. Merry Christmas."

"I'm coming up."

"I'll sick Beezus on you if you do!" I hold Beezus up to the window. Obediently he snarls. The only creature who understands me. B always has my back.

I hear the front door slam.

"You know what this means," I whisper to Beezus. "Attack mode."

Unfortunately, Bee's attack mode consists of running to my

bedroom door as it opens, sniffing Jed's motorcycle boots and letting out a trill of pure pleasure.

Jed swings Beezus into his arms. Beezus nuzzles his goatee.

Betrayed again.

"At least somebody's happy to see me," Jed says. He holds a purring Beezus high in the air. "You are the master of awesome."

Jed moves over to my bed and plonks down, a jubilant traitor of a polecat settling on his knee. He passes me a square, wrapped in newspaper.

"Merry Christmas, Mr Sardick," he says.

I maintain my silence for as long as I can. But it's too much. I can't resist a Doctor Who reference. "Christmas special, 2010. Easy one." I put Jed's gift on the bed beside me. I don't bother unwrapping it. I know what it will be. A burnt copy of whatever kooky metal act Jed is currently fixated on. His indoctrination attempts have a long history. They're also completely wasted on this nineties' pop obsessive. But you have to admire the boy's persistence.

I indicate with my head. "Yours is on the desk. Get it yourself if you want. But you'll have to ditch Judas Ferretiot to do it."

Beezus narrows his eyes. I narrow mine back.

"I'm touched." Jed grins. "But you know, I didn't come here for presents."

"It's Christmas Day."

"There's no Christmas Day in the Heartbreak Hotel."

"You. Are. A. Jerk."

"This is true. But I'm a jerk who's got a big old shoulder, just perfect for crying on. And I'm a jerk who wants to listen. Come on, Con. What happened? What was it that ended the Great Love Affair of Our Time? Viggo's not talking, so I have literally not a clue."

I grab Jed's sleeve. "Viggo's been talking to you about me? He said we had a great love affair? So does that mean he still—"

"Don't even go there," Jed interrupts. "Trust me, there's not going to be any Christmas Miracle Reunion for 'Congo'."

"Congo," I whisper, my chin trembling. "That was us. *Us.*"

We were together for a year—from December twenty-third to December twenty-third. From my birthday party last year to my …

I bury my face in my hands again. I can't think about it. I won't think about it.

"Are you thinking about it?" asks Jed. He's unwrapping his present. "Cool." I lift my head. He holds up the new, limited edition Twelfth Doctor action figure. "You know the way to a man's heart, Connie-girl. So, *were* you thinking about it?"

"Yes, *Jeremy*. I was." I wipe at my eyes. "It was my number twenty-five."

"Your … what now?"

"My twenty-five memories," I say quietly. "I told myself I was allowed twenty-five memories of Viggo—one for each Christmas chocolate in my calendar—before I wiped him from my head completely."

There's a pause. Jed raises one silver-studded eyebrow.

"Don't judge me," I mutter.

"Never would, Connie-girl. So, did it work?"

"What?"

"Is he out of your noggin?"

I shake my head, slowly. I point at my temple. "He's still there. Big time."

Jed's face softens. "Bloody Vig."

I shake my head. "Not his fault. I did it. I did everything. Viggo is perfect."

"Exactly the problem." Jed shakes his head. Then he takes my hand. "Maybe … Connie, maybe the downfall of your calendar idea is that you didn't say the memories aloud. You internalised them. You need to let them out. Talk it through. Get the feelings out into the open."

It's my turn to raise an eyebrow. This is the boy whose idea of a perfect Saturday night is a thrash concert and he's talking to me about *feelings*?

"Okay, who kidnapped Jed?" I ask. "What makes you think you're suddenly an expert on how to heal a broken heart?"

Jed shrugs. "You know what? I may not be an expert, but I have a few thoughts on you and Viggo, and I—"

I hold up a hand. "I don't want to hear them. Your thoughts. I don't want to hear how I messed up and how much I suck and how I bulldozed everything. I already know it all, Jeremiah. I am the loser-est. You don't have to tell me."

Jed gives me a funny look. "Okay, maybe I shouldn't talk at all. Maybe you need to talk instead. Maybe you should blurt it all out to the universe. The universe, in this case, being me. Consider me your Dr Freud."

"I don't want to be psychoanalysed, Jed."

"All right. Consider me your journal. Your diary. Your impartial, mute sounding board. Tell me the memories, Connie-girl."

"All twenty-five?"

Jed nods. "I have time."

"But it's Christmas. Don't you have, like, family plans?"

Jed grimaces. "Yes. I did. That's why I'm here."

I laugh, despite myself. I can only imagine what Jed's family would have arranged for Christmas evening. Jed's folks put the families in Stepford to shame.

It's no wonder Jed's sister ran off to Nimbin.

And poor, longhaired, metal-head Jed. His parents have golden hearts, but I imagine him at nighttime, under his Iron Maiden doona, dreaming of Nimbin, too.

Jed is the anti-Stepford.

Which is why it surprised me so much when Jed introduced me to Viggo. His "Other Best Friend".

Jed slung his arm around Viggo's shoulder. "This right here is Viggo Kendon MacDuff. Back from the wilderness. I hope you two get along."

I took in Viggo's button-down shirt, his pressed chinos and shiny black shoes.

I looked back at my scruffy, vampire-like friend.

And "whoa" was the first word I said to Viggo MacDuff.

"Mum was just putting on the Michael Bublé Christmas CD when I climbed out my window." Jed winces. "Please tell me stories, Connie-girl. Please give me something to do that doesn't involve eggnog and charades."

"But I ate my advent calendar ..." I gesture at the mess of chocolate-smeared cardboard on the floor. Beezus is licking it. I hope chocolate isn't bad for ferrets like it is for dogs. "I can't do the memories without the calendar!"

"Connie-girl, the lack of an advent calendar never stopped anyone reliving memories of their past loves."

"That is completely the worst epigram I have ever heard."

"I never said I was deep. I'm profoundly shallow."

"You're not allowed to quote nineties' indie pop lyrics."

"I'll do it until you tell me the memories. I got my head checked by a jumbo jet. I'm a creep. I'm a weirdo. I'm a bitch. I'm a lover. I'm a child. I'm a mother ..."

"Okay! Okay, just stop I'll tell you the damn memories."

"Every single one?"

I hug Beezus tightly and nod. "Every single memory of Viggo MacDuff."

TWO

Memory 1

"I don't really know how to do it," I admitted. "Tell the memories. I mean, a lot of it you know already."

"Pretend I don't. You'll remember it differently, anyway."

"Well, okay. This is what I remember …"

His hands were in the pockets of his ridiculously wrinkle-free chinos. He smelled of wholegrain bread and expensive aftershave. He was humming a song I vaguely recognised. From an ad on TV maybe.

"Dude, you're such a girl," Jed said, elbowing Viggo in the ribs. "What's Connie going to think of my taste in friends when I introduce you and all you can do is hum fricking Mozart?"

Viggo shrugged. "Catherine was listening to it as I left the house." He focused his bright green eyes on me. I felt dizzy. "Catherine is my sister," he explained. "She has excellent taste in all things—fashion, art … but music especially. That piece, I think you'll find, is widely regarded to be Mozart's magnum opus."

"'That piece, I think you'll find' …" Jed mimicked. He rolled his eyes at me. "You hate my other best friend already, don't you? You're going to ditch us both and go and hang out with the überclones."

I cringed. "Are you kidding me, Jeremiah? The überclones—"

As if saying their name had summoned them, Kacey Kuusela, Karen Wilson and Abigail Ward sauntered past us up the hallway, their skater skirts swishing as their hips swung from side to side. They stopped a few steps away from us, turned in perfect synchronisation, looked Viggo up and down, smiled and gave him three nauseating, fluttery-fingered waves.

I groaned inwardly. While Kacey and her fembot army had never been directly mean to me, they'd never been friendly, either. Why would they? I was a geek with no fashion sense. The fact that Kacey happened to be Em's cousin—and that Em insisted she was lovely, once you got to know her— made no difference. I still didn't exist in their world.

Luckily, I one hundred percent didn't care.

Kacey Kuusela stepped forward. She held out a Shellac-ed hand to Viggo. "Kacey Kuusela," she purred. "And you are …"

"Nice to meet you, Kacey," Viggo said. "I'm Viggo MacDuff." I glanced at his face. His smile was polite, but I could sense an undercurrent of amusement.

He shook Kacey's hand officiously and then dropped it. Kacey looked down at her fingers in surprise. She was used to boys holding on that moment too long. This was a new experience.

"So, um, you're new?" she fumbled. I couldn't help grinning. I'd never seen Kacey Kuusela ruffled before. It was a tiny bit fun.

Viggo gave a small, slow nod in reply.

"Right, well, if you need anything …"

Kacey flashed another smile—the sort of smile that knocked boys dead. The sort of smile that broke them to smithereens.

The sort of smile that seemed to have no effect whatsoever on Viggo MacDuff.

Kacey's killer grin faltered ever so slightly when she received only a polite nod in return. "Catch you soon, I hope," she said.

She returned to the others. In unison, they turned on their heels and recommenced the strut towards their glittering futures.

"Well, that was an … experience." Viggo laughed.

"*You don't think Kacey Kuusela is, like, bae AF, then?*" *Jed imitated Kacey's hair flip with his long black curls.*

"*I knew a million girls like her in Sydney,*" *Viggo said, shrugging. "All surface. Nothing at all between the ears. And they think they're the bee's knees besides. Arrogant. I don't have time for girls like that.*"

"*So you're from Sydney?*" *I asked Viggo, flinching as I realised I was asking the same sort of redundant question Kacey had just spluttered at him. "I mean,*" *I added quickly, "Jeremiah said you came from 'the wilderness'.*"

Viggo laughed. "An in-joke," *he said. "I left Tasmania when I was ten. Before that we lived down in the Huon Valley, on a small acreage, passed down through the family for generations. It was a hobby farm more than anything, but we did have a goat named Francois-Rene! It may have been far from civilisation but the aspect was quite lovely and my father made many useful renovations to the property, such as a tennis court and a heated pool. Then my mother was headhunted by a big firm in Sydney. Father told Jed we were going to 'the real jungle' and our boy believed him. The first time he came to stay I think he got something of a shock.*"

"*I wanted tigers.*" *Jed pouted.*

"*What are you complaining about?*" *Viggo flicked him on the arm. "I showed you the animals. I took you to Westfield.*"

Jed pressed a hand to his chest. "I bought my first Metallica CD at Sanity," *he sighed. "It changed my life. No zebras, though. Not even a meerkat.*"

Viggo laughed. His eyes sparkled. I was dizzy.

Disoriented.

Done for.

Oh dear. This was not good. I couldn't have a crush on Jed's best friend. How awkward would that be? And, plus, just look at him.

Viggo MacDuff had immaculately gelled blond hair and spring-grass-green eyes, and chiselled cheekbones, and an actual, honest-to-Ben-Folds cleft in his chin. He had biceps that pressed against his designer shirt, and strong hands …

And he was almost literally pulsating with success.

I was not pulsating with success.

I was barely flickering with half-hearted meh.

Viggo MacDuff was so out of my league. He was an extraordinary gentleman. I was just … Connie.

There was no chance, no hope, no—

"Galactic Republic to Connie?" Jed said, waving a skull-ringed hand past my face. I blinked.

"Huh?"

"Viggo just asked you a question."

My cheeks heated. How long had I been spacing out for? "Sorry," I mumbled. "You were saying …"

"I wanted to know if you'd like to come with me to Ronaldo's tonight?" he said, smiling dazzlingly. "Both of you. I heard the linguini there is sublime. I thought Jed and I could catch up on old times and I could get to know his other best friend a little bit better."

"I'd love to," I blurted, hoping Viggo couldn't tell just how bunny-boiling much I really would.

What in the actual Ewok was wrong with me? Why was I going all gooey over this boy? All the boys I'd crushed on before were moody, hipster musos—all dreadlocks and fedoras and retro seventies' blazers. Viggo was the complete opposite of that. So why did I feel as if I was about to keel over every time he fixed those emerald eyes on me?

"But Viggo, seriously, Ronaldo's?" Jed laughed. "Connie and I are totes Wong's Chinese people. You can go there in your pyjamas if you want to! And the number 23 is actually fricking heaven. Or, if you want to go some-where without the slight risk of salmonella poisoning, how about we try out that new retro cafe instead? Connie's been dying to go there."

It was true. I had been looking for an excuse to try the new cafe in town. It was also true that I had no idea how to dress for a place where bedwear didn't meet the dress code.

I looked at Viggo hopefully, but he just shook his head and said, "I've already made a reservation, anticipating your acceptance of my invitation.

And I'm sure Constance would not dream of wearing anything like those …" he cleared his throat, "skating shoes to Ronaldo's. I'm assuming there is an accepted attire at such an establishment. Collared shirts? Ties? Elegant formal dresses for the …" He paused and flicked his eyes my way. "Ladies?"

My face coloured again as I looked down at my Wilco tee-shirt and my Beezus-shredded jeans. Lady? Me? Hardly.

"I think a shirt might be in order," Jed admitted. "What a pity. I was going to wear my new Wintersun tee. The one with the dead guy slumped against the tree. Shame. I'll have to save that one for next time. And yeah. Might be an idea to pull those dresses out of the mothballs, Connie-girl. Hey! You could wear that Hello Kitty one. Or the one with the cherries."

I winced, thinking of the op shop frocks that were the only ones I owned. "I don't know if they'd meet the dress code either, Jed," I said.

"Why?" He shook his head. "They're awesome."

Not awesome enough for Ronaldo's. "I could borrow one from Em, I suppose," I said. I looked at Viggo. "She's my neighbour. She goes to the Catholic school. She wears dresses."

Viggo smiled. "You'd look good in a dress."

I swear my jaw hit the floor.

Was he …

He wasn't …

There was no way …

Viggo MacDuff, The Most Gorgeous Boy Alive couldn't actually be hitting on me.

Could he?

I stared at Viggo for what felt like an eternity. And Viggo stared right back, with those sparkly eyes.

And then …

"I broke the spell," Jed says. "I remember. You two were going all goo-goo eyes at each other and it was making me want to throw up my cold pizza breakfast. So I said …"

"Constance does not look good in a dress." I mimic Jed's gravelly voice. "She's got hairy legs like …"

"An exceptionally hirsute Wookie," Jed moans, smacking his forehead. He looks at me sheepishly. "You know I was just being a Dalek."

I grin. I've missed our shared habit of turning swear words into monsters from Doctor Who and Star Wars.

"I know, Jeremiah. You were worried Viggo and I would get together and leave you on the outer," I say.

Jed shakes his head. "I was worried he'd break your heart."

My grin slips. I laugh but it sounds bitter. "Well, *that* happened."

"You know, Connie, you're so much better—"

I hold up a hand. "You don't get to talk about Viggo," I say. "Remember? This is my time for talking." Just then, my belly lets out a long, loud grumble. "Except enough talking for now. All I've had to eat today is twenty-five advent calendar chocolates."

"But it's Christmas …"

"Exactly," I say. "So, you want to go to Wong's?"

THREE

Wong's is Bangarra's local all-you-can-eat twenty-four-hour Chinese buffet. It's cheap and it's greasy and that's exactly why Jed and I love it.

And why Viggo hates it.

I haven't been to Wong's for more than a year; not since Viggo swaggered into my life and swept me away.

I stopped wearing my Joe Cool Vans.

I stopped staying in my pyjamas until lunchtime on a weekend, watching old Recovery videos on YouTube and eating microwave waffles.

I stopped reading graphic novels ("glorified comic books").

I stopped dyeing pink and green bits in my hair.

I stopped singing along at the top of my voice to cheesy nineties' pop songs on commercial radio.

I stopped spending my entire income on music magazines, art supplies and crazy outings with Jed.

And Viggo thinks Wong's is an abomination. So I stopped eating there.

But now Viggo MacDuff hates my guts, so I can eat as much Szechuan prawn and fried ice cream as I like.

Jed is happy. "I've missed coming to this place with you," he says as he loads up his plate with rice and sweet and sour chicken.

"You still come here?" I ask, surprised. I thought Jed gave up Wong's when I did. "But Viggo hates it."

"Viggo also hates Iron Maiden, facial piercings and boots." Jed gestures down at his tee-shirt and clompy shoes. He raises an eyebrow and his silver stud sparkles. "And all manner of other awesome things. And I actually don't give much of a Flying Millennium Falcon what Viggo hates." He nods at my feet. "I'm glad the Snoop Dog Vans have made a return. You really never were a high heels sort of girl."

"I tried," I say, sinking into a red plastic chair. "I tried heels and skirts and a ponytail and clever books and fancy wine and no Wong's …"

"I'm glad you're back." Jed grins.

"I'm not," I mumble. "Not if it means Viggo hates me."

"Well, I don't think you should give a rat's a—"

"Jed!"

"All right. Sorry. I forgot. No Jed talking. Only Connie talking. So spill already."

"I need more satay squid first," I say, smiling to make up for the snappishness. "Ben Folds, I miss this place."

"I miss you saying Ben Folds instead of 'God'."

We walk together back to the buffet. "I never said 'God' when I was with Viggo either. It's—"

"Blasphemous and uncouth," we say, in unison.

"God, *isn't* it?" I say, smiling.

"Good to see you smile," says Jed. And that what makes the smile fall off. Because I remember why I wasn't smiling before.

"Are you ready to tell me your next one?"

I nod and wipe black bean sauce from my mouth with the back of my hand.

Viggo hated it when I did that, too.

Uncouth ...

"My next one is the night we went to Ronaldo's. Do you—" I catch Jed's expression. "Oh. Right."

Jed shrugs. "My two best friends getting together? Of course a guy would remember that."

"But we didn't get together that night."

Jed snorts. "Far from it, if I recall."

I look down at my plate. "It wasn't my finest hour, I'll admit."

"And yet he fell for you. Of course."

I look up at Jed. He has rice stuck in his beard. It would be kind of cute, if it wasn't *Jed*.

And, like a kick to the gut, I remember one time I had a brioche crumb on my cheek and Viggo wiped it away and his fingertips were so gentle ...

Oh *Ben Folds* I miss him.

"Jed," I begin quietly. "Do you really think there's no chance—"

"Just tell the story, Connie," Jed says at the same time. "I know I remember it like it was yesterday but it will still be hilarious hearing *you* relive it." He picks up his fork again—unlike Viggo, Jed is hopeless with chopsticks—and stabs a chunk of chicken. "Come on, Connie-girl. Entertain me."

"So I wore a dress ..."

"I remember. *Trust* me." Jed waggles his eyebrows. "No man alive could forget your Ronaldo's dress."

I punch him on the arm. "Shut up, cretin. As if you could ever think of me as anything other than geeky old Connie-girl. Besides, you made fun of me all night in that dress. And *besides*, it wasn't *my* Ronaldo's dress, anyway, was it? It was Em's. And that just made it *worse*."

"I'd forgotten about that. And here was I thinking it couldn't *get* any worse ..."

"I should have known then, Jed." My eyes burn. "I should have known right then that I would never be good enough for Viggo. I'm not good enough for anyone."

Jed's jaw twitches. "Enough of that, okay, Connie? Why don't you just tell the story?"

"Okay." My voice cracks. I take a sip of water. My skull feels hollowed out. Everything feels hollow. I feel like I'm weightless, floating through space. I feel like I'm nothing.

"Connie. You don't have to—"

But I do. I do. Because what else can I do?

"I'll start from when I borrowed the dress from Em."

"Oh, goody." Jed rubs his hands together. "You just *know* how much I love fashion talk."

I roll my eyes. "I went over to Emily's after school ..."

"Wait on," Jed holds up a hand. "Can you describe this 'Emily' for me?"

"You've met her before, like, a zillion times."

Jed's lip flickers. "Well, yeah, but Connie, the girl is, like, Karen-Gillan-level hot." Karen Gillan is Jed's favourite *Doctor Who* companion, and also his biggest celebrity crush of all time. "I'm looking forward to the mental image!"

I groan but I'm finally smiling again. "Because my only goal in life is creating sexy mental images for my best friend."

"Humour me."

I puffed out my lips. "So, Emily Chambers is approximately one hundred and seventy-five centimetres tall ..."

FOUR

Memory 2

She's also beautiful. Not just "hot". Not just contour and bodycon dresses. Like, supermodel-movie-star-actual-angel beautiful.

If she wasn't so gosh-darn nice, it would be all too easy to hate Emily Chambers.

But Emily has the heart of a Disney princess. Also, she genuinely doesn't seem to notice how exquisite she is—a hangover, so her mum told me, of having been skinny and gawky and awkward until she hit puberty and turned into a swan.

I didn't know Em back then. We only became friends when her family moved next door when we were both in grade seven. Mum made me go over to the Chambers' house the day after the moving truck left, with a dish of Thermomix stew. I was reluctant. I'd been covertly spying on Emily for the past two days and I knew someone with looks like that would never want me for a friend.

Besides, I didn't need another friend.

I had Jed.

"Aww."

"Me talking."

"Soz."

I was relieved when nobody answered my knocking, and I left the dish on the front deck with a hastily scrawled note: "From the Chases at Number Five. Welcome."

I thought I'd escaped but, the next afternoon, as I sat at the kitchen table reading Watchmen, the doorbell rang.

I opened the door to a beaming goddess carrying a gingham-covered tray of something that smelled so good my belly gave out a long, low growl.

The goddess laughed. "Sounds like I arrived at just the right time." She held out the tray. "Blueberry muffins. Freshly baked. I made them to say thank you for the stew. Your dish is in the dishwasher. Maybe you can come over later and collect it and we can hang out? I'm Emily Chambers, by the way."

"Constance Chase. Most people call me Connie."

"Constance! Like Constance Adams." When I returned a blank look, Emily went on. "She's an architect. And she works on the space program. She designs living quarters for astronauts. My parents are architects," she explained.

"Actually, I'm named after Connie Smith," I explained, fully expecting a blank stare right back at me. Instead, Emily clicked her fingers.

"The country singer, right?"

I felt my eyebrows hit my dyed-pink fringe. "You know her?"

Emily shrugged. "My dad loves country music. It's rubbed off on me over the years. Much to my mum's horror. Although, really, I'm more of an indie girl."

"Nineties?" I asked hopefully.

She shook her head. "Current, mostly. Triple J stuff. But nineties is cool too."

"Awesome!" I couldn't help smiling. I was warming to my new neighbour, despite myself.

"I have to admit, though, I don't listen to as much music as I should," Emily said. "I mostly listen to it while I'm doing my art."

"I love art!" I cried, any hint of coolness melted. "I want to be a graphic novelist!"

"I want to be an abstract artist like Jackson Pollock!" Emily squealed. And then …

"Ahem."

Jed is regarding me across the table, his fingers steepled below his chin.

"What?"

"Okay, I know it was me who asked for a description of Princess Charming, but I was thinking a fifty-word synopsis, not a whole novel. We're meant to be talking about my man, Vig, aren't we? Are you procrastinating, Connie-girl? Do you not want to talk about Viggo anymore?"

There's a long silence that fills my head with noise. Finally, I manage, "I *miss* him."

"It's only been, like, two days."

"Longest two days ever."

"You two were apart for longer when he went with his family to Venice."

"We weren't *together* then," I point out.

"You were together when he went to Auckland for the Future Leaders conference."

"True … but we talked every night on the phone." I lick sauce from my thumb. It tasted good when I was eating the noodles. Now it seems greasy and salty and bad. My stomach turns. "I held the fort back here for him. I ran errands and … I knew he still liked me."

"Liked you? Don't you mean *loved* you?"

"Yeah, that's what I mean," I mumble. I'm not really lying.

I know he *felt* it.

I knew it was only a matter of time before he said it, too. It's my fault. I shouldn't have said it when he was about to go on stage to give his speech for winning male dux at the end of year assembly. I caught him off guard.

He was distracted.

He would have said it back if he wasn't distracted.

He—

"Connie?" Jed is clicking his fingers. "The story? Ronaldo's? We'll be here all night if you don't get started, and much as I love Wong's chicken for breakfast ..."

"Okay," I say. "Time for the proper story. Time for Ronaldo's."

FIVE

"So, I borrowed a dress from Emily," I say quickly. "She was all excited because she convinced herself I had a date with you—you know how she's bizarrely obsessed with us getting together …" I roll my eyes.

"It's in the stars …" Jed says breathily, wiggling his fingers.

"No, Emily isn't silly enough to believe in astrology," I correct him. "It's some personality matrix psychology thing she did, remember? Anyway, I'm getting distracted already. So, she thought we had a date, even though I *told* her there was someone else coming …"

"Yeah, but he's just some friend of Jed's, right?" Emily said. "Jed's probably just invited him because he's nervous about being alone with you."

"Jed and I spend half our lives alone together," I pointed out, flopping on Emily's bed. She was already inside her enormous wardrobe-room-thing. It was groaning with frills and ruffles and peplums. She was going to make me look like a toilet dolly. "Besides, it was Viggo who suggested the dinner."

"Perfect cover for Jed's cunning plan." Emily emerged with an armful of brightly coloured fabric scraps.

"Em, not one of them is knee-length, is it?"

Em grinned wickedly. "Fair maiden never won the heart of sexy Jed wearing knee-length skirt."

"Wait." Jed holds up a hand. "Emily Chambers thinks I'm sexy?"

"Did I say sexy? I meant sleazy. Shut up. *So,* after, like, an hour of trying on handkerchiefs I finally settled on the one I wore. The red one."

"The Princess-Leia-level hot one."

"Whatever. And Em made me wear heels too ..."

SIX

Memory 3

I could barely walk in the heels. I had to lean on Jed the whole way from the car park to the restaurant.

Which Emily said was totally the point.

Viggo was already waiting for us when we got inside. "I forgot he's always annoyingly early," Jed grumbled. "For Viggo, 'late' is arriving on time."

Viggo had—somehow—managed to wangle the best table in the restaurant. I had no idea how—the place was packed. I'd heard you had to make bookings months in advance.

"The man's a legend," Jed said, shrugging as we walked in. "I swear, he could sell awesome to Iron Maiden."

I waited.

"You know the saying?" he went on, understanding the question mark my raised eyebrow was making. "Sell ice to the Eskimos? Or Inuits or whatever? Well, Iron Maiden have, like, the most awesome in the whole world, but Viggo could sell them more."

We were nearly at the table now. Viggo had spotted us and was standing up from the table.

Standing up.

To greet us.

Who did that? Who didn't just, like, wave? Or text "hi".

"Your analogy sucks," I murmured, nodding at Viggo in greeting.

"At least my vocabulary is creative," Jed shot back. "I mean, really, 'sucks'? Aren't you meant to be the English nerd?"

"Who's the English nerd?" Viggo asked.

Jed pulled out my chair for me. He always did that. It was one of his "things".

"I am," I replied. "Thanks, Jeremiah." I sat down.

"Oh, yes, Jed said you're quite the scholar." Viggo smiled, his eyes glimmering like a summer ocean. "And you could be dux of the school if you only 'applied yourself'."

"I was quoting your teachers," Jed said, rolling his eyes. "I was being sarcastic. Viggo doesn't understand sarcasm."

"In any case, it impressed me, Constance. It's part of the reason I was so intrigued to meet you. A girl with brains is difficult to find these days. And one who looks rather fetching in a nice frock! And might I say, I'm glad you chose a sensible length of skirt. So rare these days."

"You wouldn't have liked the dresses Emily wanted me to wear, then!" I smiled and picked up the menu. It was huge—so many delicious choices! Lucky Mum and Dad were shouting me.

"Ben Folds, I have no idea what to order!" I gasped. "The pizzas look amazing, but then there's the risotto and—oh—should we have bruschetta to start? Then, oh my God, I am so having gelati to finish, but chocolate or lemon? And—"

"Relax!" Viggo pulled the menu gently from my grasp. "I've saved you the quandary of deciding. I got here early and spoke to the chef- turns out he's an old high school friend of Dad's. He's making us all a special, off-the-menu feast! Veal ziti and squid ink fettuccini and Torta alla Monferrina for dessert." He kissed his fingertips. "It will be belissimo!"

I gaped at him, lost for words. For one thing, I didn't eat veal—it was cruel. For another, squid ink pasta? Yuck! For another …

Ziti sounded like it might involve pus.

"You've gone white," Jed teased. He turned to Viggo. "Connie-girl's more of a Hawaiian pizza chick, dude. And I know for a fact she doesn't eat veal."

"Well, I'll let her choose her own entree then," Viggo conceded. "But she has to have the fettuccini. And the torta is to die for. Trust me, you'll thank me, Constance."

"Um, okay," I said, looking dubiously at Jed. "God, um, thanks …"

Jed laughed. "You'll soon learn my best friend doesn't really take 'no' for an answer. He likes to be right. Almost as much as he hates it when people say 'God'."

My hand flew to my mouth. "Really? Are you religious? I'm so sorry."

Viggo shook his head. "I'm an atheist. But I still believe that using the word 'God' as a cuss is blasphemous and uncouth. Besides, I'm sure a girl with your English skills could come up with a much more creative expletive to use in its place."

He smiled kindly, and I felt less embarrassed. I felt as if I was glowing.

He could give me as many of those smiles as he wanted.

I cleared my throat. "Golly? Gosh? Gee-whizz? Egad? But I do tend to go with Ben Folds as an alternative to 'God', most of the time. He's God in my world."

Viggo's brows knitted in confusion.

"Ben Folds?" I repeated. "Of Ben Folds Five fame? Only one of the greatest singers, songwriters and pianists of all time?"

When Viggo still looked clueless, Jed helped. "'Brick'? 'Underground'? 'Kate'?"

Viggo shook his head. "Yes, to me that simply sounds like a random collection of words. But as you know, I'm more of a classical man myself. None of this mainstream music business for me." He gestured at Jed's Nightwish satchel.

"Nightwish. Are. Not. Mainstream," Jed said through gritted teeth.

I've known Jed long enough to have witnessed more than one shouting match as a result of calling his favourite band "mainstream", so I was glad when, just then, the entrees arrived.

Viggo had the veal ziti (which, thankfully, looked exactly like spaghetti and nothing like a dermatological disease), but Jed had bruschetta too. "You've got me thinking about the poor little calves," he said, grimacing. "You're turning me soft, Connie-girl!"

As we ate, Viggo and Jed reminisced about old times. Viggo told a story about how he won so many primary school awards that his bedroom over-flowed with trophies. Jed offered to store some of them in his bedroom. "My grandmother came over one day and completely confused the p's by saying how proud she was that I'd won all this stuff!" Jed laughed. "Mum and Dad didn't have the heart to correct her."

"Always riding on my coat-tails, weren't you, Jeremy?" Viggo said, laughing.

By the time we'd cleaned our plates, the talk had moved on to the present, and Bangarra High School.

"I think I'll fit in perfectly," Viggo said. "Plenty of clubs to join, plenty of stimulating extracurriculars. What clubs are you involved with, Constance?" Viggo fixed me with those eyes and smiled again. I blushed as I exchanged a look with Jed. How could I explain to Captain Success that the only clubs I was in were the Manga society, the school band and the creative writing group? Even though the last one was invitation-by-teacher-only, none of them screamed "academia".

"We are in our own Club of Awesome," Jed said, as I mumbled, "Well, it's early in the year so I haven't actually firmed up ..."

Viggo rubbed his hands together. "That's excellent! A blank canvas! We can join some clubs together. Tell me, Constance, how do you feel about Australian politics?"

"Well, I, um—" I didn't know what to say. I mean, I cared about poli-tics, sure. I'd already decided I was going to vote Green when I turned eigh-teen, but something told me Viggo was not a Greens-voter, and Dad was always telling me you shouldn't discuss sex or politics when on a date ...

Not that we were on a date ...

Had I really just thought about talking sex with Viggo MacDuff?

My face was turning the colour of my bruschetta.

Again, I was saved by the meal. I started to breathe a sigh of relief …

Then I saw it.

It was black.

It was a big, slimy plate of black.

It reminded me—stomach-turningly—of the wobbly tentacles attached to the faces of the Ood in Doctor Who.

I held a hand to my mouth. The walls of Ronaldo's seemed to wobble.

Viggo rubbed his hands together. "Oh yes. This is what I've been waiting for!"

Jed laughed. "It looks like entrails."

My stomach heaved.

"Or …!" Jed twirled some around his fork. "You know that Japanese movie, The Grudge?" I shuddered as I remembered the terrifying horror film we'd watched together a year ago. "It looks like Sadako's hair—the ghost girl, remember? Don't you think, Connie? Or—or, I know! Connie, you'll love this! It looks like when Beezus ate that dead, rotten fish at the beach and then threw it up and … Um, Connie? You've gone kind of a funny colour."

Jed was talking in slow motion.

The room was lurching like a ship on stormy seas.

I was vaguely aware of Viggo looking at me with concern, but his face was all fuzzy.

My stomach contracted one final time, bringing my bruschetta up all over me …

And Emily's dress …

The plate of squid ink pasta …

The table …

And a bit on Viggo MacDuff's hand.

"Oh my God," I moaned. "I mean, not God. I mean …"

Viggo was looking between me and his vomit-sodden cuff in total shock.

Jed held a hand over his mouth to stop himself laughing.

"I'm so sorry," I whispered, tears burning in my eyes. "Your shirt."

I wanted the Doctor to come in his Tardis and take me to another planet. Even if it was one with Daleks or even the Weeping Angels. Even if it was one that was about to implode in an hour, killing all beings that walked upon it. I didn't care. I just wanted to go.

But then, just as I was preparing to push back my chair and run from the restaurant into the street, Viggo did the thing that made my sad little crush on him turn into something more.

"It's only a shirt," he said, looking down at the cuff. "In fact, it's only a shirt I don't like very much. My sister Catherine bought it for me online. I mean, just because it's a Tom Ford shirt and cost two hundred dollars … that's beside the point. The point is, are you all right?"

My heart swelled.

He didn't care about the shirt. He cared about Me.

The thing is, I'd never really had a boy care about me before. Apart from Jed, of course, but he didn't count. He was Jed. He wasn't a boy, to me. Not a proper, gorgeous, green-eyed, smart, high-achieving, floppy-haired, beautiful boy …

Like Viggo MacDuff.

Of course I cared that Jed cared. I loved that he did little things to show it, like buying me Ben Folds memorabilia when it came up on eBay, or bringing me Wong's takeaway when I was sick. That was awesome. And I thought he was the bee's knees, but to have beautiful Viggo care …

Wow.

"Um, thanks …" I murmured.

Viggo passed me his fabric serviette. "You might want to give yourself a little wipe-down," he said gently. "You're a bit—"

"Covered … in … spew …" Jed could barely talk, he was laughing so hard.

What was I saying about caring? Slitheen-head.

"I'll order you another main, if you feel up to eating," Viggo went on. "Whatever you like. As long as it's not Hawaiian pizza."

I nodded. "Chicken pizza?" I said quietly. "It's free-range."

"Connie cares about that stuff," Jed said. "Animals and stuff. She isn't only a vomiting weirdo."

I poked my tongue out at him.

"A social conscience can be a valuable attribute." Viggo smiled. "If channelled wisely. Good girl, Constance!"

"I'm a girl who's covered in vomit," I said mournfully. "I'm a wreck."

Viggo raised an eyebrow. "We'll take care of that," he said. "We'll fix you."

SEVEN

J ed and I are walking back to my place from Wong's.

Tallulah, Jed's ancient, beaten-up old Gemini, is "resting" in the Wong's car park and, since it's Boxing Day (and also nearly midnight), there are no buses. Luckily, Wong's is only a half-hour walk from home, so I'm not hating Jed too much.

I'm too busy hating myself.

"It's not helping," I mutter.

"Talking about Viggo?"

I nod. "It's just making me think about him more and how much I miss him and how badly I stuffed up."

"Was what you did really so bad?"

I nod mutely.

My body is exploding with the pain of it. Everything inside of me aches for Viggo.

"Connie?" Jed reaches out to touch me and I flinch instinctively away.

I place a protective hand on my ribs. "I'm sorry," I whisper. "I miss him so much. And at the same time, it was like it was never even real, you know? Like a dream."

"Like finding a TARDIS in the middle of the Bangarra Mall?" Jed smiles. And I can't help smiling, a bit.

"Yeah, like that."

It's just one of our many ideas for how to escape Bangarra and our own ennui. Amongst others: starting the world's first nineties' indie pop/power metal fusion band; or directing a film in which Daleks appear in Tasmania and start attacking people at Salamanca market and are taken down by an army of Ewoks who've joined forces with a pack of mutant Tasmanian Devils; or creating a new superfood …

We're not even sure what our superfood will be, only that it will be glittery and we'll get Karen Gillan from Doctor Who to endorse it and we'll make *one million dollars.*

I never told Viggo about our plans. He would have thought they were stupid.

Because they are.

Viggo is sensible. Viggo is *mature.* Viggo cares about things that matter.

He used to care about me too.

And now he is *gone, gone, gone,* like just about every nineties' band that was ever any good. And he won't be coming back because the only nineties' bands that ever come back are crap ones like Steps and S Club 7.

I *miss him* like you miss a really good dream, when you wake up to reality.

My wallowing is rudely interrupted as my feet move from crunchy gravel to soft sand.

There is no sand on the way to my house.

"Jed, where have you taken us?" I peer around in the darkness. I can see the moon reflected off gentle waves. I can hear splashing and seagulls and, distantly, a dog howling.

We're not in Kansas anymore, Toto.

Or anywhere near my house.

"You really were in your own little world," Jed says.

"My own planet."

"Planet Viggo?"

I sigh. "Yup. But now I am back from Planet Viggo and I appear to be at the seaside."

"Or, as I like to call it, Planet Jed." Jed grins.

"Explain."

Jed takes my hand and breaks into a run. "What in the actual Cyberman?" I yell as I race—against my will—towards the jet-black waves. Jed doesn't answer. As we get closer and closer to the border between sand and surf I realise something horrifying.

Jed isn't going to stop.

We are going *in* the water.

Sure it's summer, but it's still *Tasmania*. And it's *midnight*.

I'm fully clothed.

Yes, I may be clothed in my "Viggo-dumped-me-my-world-is-over-why-bother-dressing-like-a-respectable-human-being outfit of my oldest jeans and moth-eaten Regurgitator tee-shirt, but I *am* also wearing my Vans.

My *Vans!*

I haven't worn my Vans for over a year. I do not want them all filled up with water and sand and seaweed! I don't care what Jed's plan is, or why he wants to submerge me in the freezing sea early on Boxing Day morning. I may love Jed dearly but I am *not sacrificing my favourite shoes*.

"Jed! Jed!" I cry.

"Not stopping, Connie-girl!"

"My *Vans!*" I scream. Jed stops abruptly.

I keep going.

Jed is still holding my hand.

I lasso backwards, landing on my bottom on the sand.

I look up at Jed. "Seriously? Ow."

"Take off your kicks."

"Why do you even want to go in the—"

"Take off your Vans, Connie."

"I don't even get why you—"

"Oh my Actual Bruce Dickinson." Jed flops on the sand beside me and covers his face with his hands. "What has Viggo MacDuff done to my best friend?" he groans through his fingers.

"Nothing! These are just my favourite and my best!" I pull Jed's hands away from his face and point at my toes. "See?"

"Were you wearing your lo pros when I suggested we go and see Foster and Allen play the casino?"

"Well, no, but Viggo was worried you'd incite me to heckling. Or, worse, playing Foster-and-Allen-themed drinking games and then encouraging my drunk self to get up on stage and dance with Foster. Or Allen. And then snog them."

"Viggo thought that?" Jed looks incredulous. I nod. "The man knows me too well," Jed mutters. He sits up. "I know you weren't wearing your Vans the day I suggested we hijack the school assembly by paying Craig Flemish to play Megadeth's *Symphony of Destruction* instead of the school song. You were, as I remember, wearing shiny black shoes with bows on them. Did Viggo make you buy those, by the way? They were beyond lame. You looked like you belonged on the Disney Channel."

"Shut up," I mumble. "And no, he did not *make* me buy them. He might have *suggested* it, but that's not the same thing. And also, in point of fact, I did say I'd consider your plan if we got Craig to play *Rockin' the Suburbs* instead of Megadeth."

"I knew you didn't mean it. You would've chickened out at the last minute. You would have found some excuse. Like now with the shoes. Face it, Connie, Viggo ruined you."

I punch Jed on the arm. "I am *so* not ruined."

"Prove it."

"How?"

Jed groans. "See? The Connie Chase I know would have said

'okay' before she said 'how'? Viggo MacDuff sucked out your spirit like an überclone drinking a Diet Coke." When I open my mouth to protest, Jed holds up a hand. "Please say you'll let go a bit, Connie-girl. Please. Otherwise, I'm not sure we can ever go back to being best friends."

I think for a moment.

I look out at the ocean. It does actually look kind of nice tonight—all sparkly and magical under the moonlight. "One condition. No, scratch that, two."

Jed puffs out an exhausted breath. "Go on."

"One: you stop saying bad stuff about Viggo. There is nothing bad about Viggo. He is perfect. Okay?"

"I'll agree with you on that one. Viggo is perfect. But that's not necessarily a good thing, so—"

"Agree or I walk." Jed nods reluctantly. "Right, second ... I don't want to be Diet Coke."

"Huh?" Jed raises an eyebrow.

"You said the überclone drank me like Diet Coke. You know I hate Diet Coke."

Jed sits up and meets my eyes. "Connie, you might not want to hear it, but while you were with Viggo you kind of became Diet Coke."

Jed catches the wobble in my chin.

"Okay, Connie-girl, if you go along with my perfect plan I have to de-Viggo you, then you get to be a lime spider," Jed promises. "I know you love lime spiders."

"Do I still have to do my twenty-five memories?"

Jed nods. "Twenty-three, I think it is now. And yes, I think you should do the memories as well as my stuff. I think it will ... help. In fact, I think we're due for the next one."

"Okay." I lie back on the sand. "You'll like this one, anyway. It involves Emily again."

"By the way, you know how I went on about how Emily's hot?" Jed says, lying down beside me. "I was just trolling you."

"It's okay." I throw him a sideways look. "You don't need to apologise. Em's everything. She's perfect, just like Viggo. They're the same. And we're the same."

"Imperfect people?" Jed gives a half grin.

"Yeah. But you're still awesome."

"So are you. I love your imperfections."

"Of which there are many, as we have established. But are we going to talk all night about how defective I am, or do you want to hear me talk?"

"I want to hear you talk," Jed says. "I'm not Viggo MacDuff."

EIGHT

*M*emory 3
I went over to Em's house with Beezus after school. Emily has her own ferret, called Ferretto Rocher. Bee and Ro have regular play dates. They're brothers from another mother.

While they bonded, Emily and I made huge mugs of Milo and cold milk, loaded up our plates with Emily's famous sultana scones, and dissected our days. Emily asked me the same first question every time we caught up:

"So, have you kissed Jeremy yet?"

"I've told you a million times, he prefers 'Jed'," I said, reaching over to wipe away Em's milk moustache. "And I've also told you a million times, the likelihood of me and Jed getting together is about equal to finding the Tardis in the middle of the Bangarra mall."

"Stranger things have happened," Jed interrupts. "We can dream. One day there will be a TARDIS just for us …"

"Jed?"

"Yep? Oh, okay. Sorry. You talking. Please resume."

Emily sighed. "It's tragic you feel that way. You two are destined."

I changed the subject. "So, how goes it at St Snooty's?"

Emily rolled her eyes. "Same old. This year is no different from any other year. Same tragic uniforms. Same depressingly healthy canteen food.

Same pressure to be excellent at all of the everything. Oh, there is one good thing, though: they've started offering a new sculpture elective, and I convinced Mum to let me ditch Advanced Calculus to enrol. I think she's finally coming around to the idea that I'll be studying Fine Arts at uni, not architecture. Yay for life goals. You and me, kid. We'll both rule the art world. The world is our oyster. Which, by the way, is such a weird expression, isn't it? Like, who wants an oyster, really?"

Thinking about oysters made me think about squid ink, which made me think (after a brief wave of nausea) about Viggo.

Thinking of Viggo made me blush.

Emily giggled. "Look at those cheeks! You are so thinking of Jeremy and how you secretly love him."

"I am so ... not," I said truthfully.

"You paused. You're thinking about Jed!" Emily pulled back her spoon and flicked Milo at me. It hit me, conveniently, on the mouth.

I licked it off. "Yum. Thanks, Em. But I am not thinking of Jed."

Em narrowed her eyes. "Someone else then?"

"No. Well ..."

And just at that moment my phone buzzed.

Saved by the ringtone.

I held up a finger as Emily stage-whispered, "Is it Jeremy?"

I frowned down at my phone. "Unknown number." Tentatively, I answered. "Connie's phone. You may talk if you are the shit."

"But you won't be for long," Em whisper-sang. This is why she's my best friend—she recognises all the Ben Folds references.

I heard laughter down the line. "Well, that is certainly an unconventional phone manner, Constance Chase."

A whistling noise started in my ears. I felt hot and cold and like I needed to sit down.

Right. Now.

Viggo MacDuff was on my telephone. And I had just sworn and referenced an obscure indie pop song from 2003.

Emily noticed the look on my face. "What?" she whispered.

I shook my head at her. I sat, shakily, on one of her kitchen stools. I put my phone on the table and looked down at it.

"Who is it? Say something, weirdo!" Emily hissed. Viggo's tinny "Hello, Constance? Hello?" could be heard faintly coming from the table top.

"He sounds hot," Emily hissed. "For pity's sake, say something, Con!"

I gulped, took a deep breath and picked up my phone again. "Sorry about that, Viggo," I said. "I—um—my ferret took my phone."

Emily dropped her head to her hands. I wanted to be swallowed whole by some sort of enormous, temporarily land-dwelling sea creature.

"Con! Connie!" Emily was snapping her fingers in front of my face. She pointed at my ear, where I could hear Viggo chatting away about … something. I realised he'd been talking for at least a minute and I hadn't heard a single word he'd said.

"… Constance? Does that sound feasible?"

I cleared my throat. "Um, okay?"

I had no idea what I was agreeing to. Viggo could be asking me if "Barbie Girl" by Aqua was the best song of the nineties.

He could be asking me to give away my Ben Folds Five CD collection or my complete set of Doctor Who DVDs, or to stop wearing my Snoopy Vans and dyeing my hair crazy colours.

I had no clue whatsoever. All I knew was that, when Viggo MacDuff asked me to do something, I was inclined to say "yes".

"Excellent. So, Friday night then?"

I looked, wide-eyed, at Em. "What?" she mouthed. When I didn't respond, she hissed, "Speak!"

I took a deep breath. "Yep Friday night awesomesauce see you then bye now all righty buh bye," I blurted and quickly pressed the hang-up button, dropping my phone on the table as if it was made of hot coal.

"So. Not. Jeremy," Emily said slowly.

I shook my head. "Not Jeremy."

"Jeremy's Other Best Friend?"

I nodded silently.

"Hottie MacHotterson."

"MacDuff," I corrected her quietly. I knew my cheeks were the colour of the raspberry jam Emily was slowly spreading on her scone, while never taking her narrowed eyes off me. "Viggo MacDuff."

"You like the boy," she said sagely.

"He's ... pretty," I admitted. I cringed. "When did I become the girl who cared about that? I thought I liked indie musos with messy bed-hair and dorky glasses and too-tight Goodies tee-shirts. I thought I liked boys who smelled faintly of sweat and cigarettes and had bags under their eyes from playing gigs late at night. I thought I liked boys who disappeared for days on end while they wrote songs about girls called Georgia and rode around on vintage bicycles and only listened to vinyl and—"

"Enough." Emily held her butter knife to my throat. "You like the boy?"

I nodded. "He's smart, too. And polite and, like, refined."

Emily's forehead creased. "He sounds ... fun."

"Wait until you see his eyes ..." I giggled. "They are dreamy."

"Well, then." Emily took a bite of scone. "Why didn't you say so? No more need be said. Dreamy eyes? We have to find you a dress."

NINE

We're at my place now. We walked back from the beach. Thankfully in dry, warm clothes. Jed eventually came to his senses and realised it was actually too freezing. And that he liked his own biker boots too much to get them wet either.

We're sitting on my front deck.

We may or may not also be drinking lime spiders. I just couldn't get the idea out of my head and then Jed *made* me make them because, apparently, I "mentioned them fifty times in the space of half an hour."

He said it could be the first of his "Adventures".

The adventures are, he says, his foolproof means of curing me of heartbreak. And he has enough of them, apparently, for each of the rest of my memories of Viggo MacDuff.

The first one is to drink a lime spider.

"You are aware this is not a very adventurous adventure," I point out, gesturing at our glasses. "You know nothing comes between me and junk food."

"Except for Viggo MacDuff," Jed replied. "Have you forgotten already? The boy would only let you eat multigrain bread. And no butter, only *Tahiti*."

"Tahini," I correct him. "And he never *made* me. I just ... wanted to try something different. But now I have decided—all by myself—that I do not like tahini and I would like fizzy lime cordial and ice cream instead. It has nothing to do with Viggo."

"All righty then," says Jed. For a moment there's silence as we eat. Then Jed says, "Well, hopefully, the more fizzy cordial you drink the better these 'memories' will get, because so far they're sucking."

"It's just what happened!" I protest.

"Then what happened is *boring!*" Jed exclaims through a mouthful of ice-cream. Some spits on the floor. The boy is all class. "Seriously, I was after juicy dirt on the V man. And what I'm getting is, 'Oh, this one time he called me on my mobile phone when I was at my neighbour's house and I sang a song'. Really? *Really*, Connie? Was your relationship that unexciting that, out of a whole entire year, *that* is what you remember?"

"It was a pivotal moment," I mumble. "Our first phone call. It was important. But there were many more significant and sensational memories. They are still to come. Besides, you are the boy who thinks drinking spiders is an adventure."

"Like you, I am starting small," Jed says. "Plus, you know, a spider is soft drink *plus ice-cream*. That's pretty damn adventurous, Con. *Pretty damn adventurous.*"

"Your life is nearly as sad as mine," I murmur sympathetically.

"Nope. I wasn't dumped by The Perfect Man. Loser."

I whack Jed around the side of his messy dark head. "And here I was feeling sorry for you for a second."

"First time for everything, I suppose," Jed says.

"What's that supposed to mean?" I examine Jed's face. There is no trace of his usual cheeky grin. He looks almost ... glum. "Jed?" I press. "What do you mean?"

"Nothing," he mumbles, digging the toe of his biker boot in the dirt. "Are you going to tell me another memory or not?"

I put down my spoon. I'm suddenly not hungry. Something is up with Jed and I need to know what it is.

"Jed, I know it's not nothing," I say. "I know you. I know when something's not right."

"Oh yeah?" Jed looks up at me, and the expression on his face is accusing, angry even.

Why is Jed angry at *me?*

Why is everyone angry at me?

Beezus leaps from Jed's lap on to the table. She can sense tension and she doesn't like it. She skitters across to me and plops on my knee, burying her little pink nose in the folds of my hoodie.

"You scared Beezus," I say. "By being all angry. I thought you said you *weren't* angry at me about stuffing up with Viggo."

"Not everything is about Viggo!" Jed's voice is raised. His eyes are blazing. He breathes out, shakily. "Forget it. Just forget it, Connie, okay? I'm sorry. Tonight *is* about Viggo. It's about you and Viggo and your memories of him and you getting over him. Just forget the last five minutes ever happened, okay? My bad. So talk."

"Okay," I say slowly. "But are you sure—"

"Drop it, Constance," Jed says, but his voice is calmer now. "Please? All I want in the whole world is for you to entertain me some more with another of your hilarious anecdotes about receiving phone calls."

"I don't *only* have phone-call anecdotes," I protest. "Aren't you curious about what happened that Friday night?"

"Actually …"

I raise my eyebrows, expectantly.

"No," Jed finishes. "But you might surprise me."

"Oh fine. But I need the toilet first. Here, hold Beezus. Don't feed her any more waffles." I pass a bundle of floppy ferret over to my frustrating best friend and go inside. On my way back outside, the phone rings. "Who in Ben Folds' name rings at this time of the night-slash-morning?" I mutter as I pace over to the phone. I check my watch. It's past one am.

If I was the optimistic type, of course I'd think it was Viggo, but Viggo's never up this late. Also, he hates me. Also, I am not the optimistic type. So I know it's not him.

Only one way to find out. "Speak, if you are big and important, or kiss my ass goodbye."

"Well, that's a lovely way to greet your favourite next-door-neighbour. Although I am pleased to hear the Ben Folds references have made a welcome return, post-Viggo."

"Em!" There's a lump, all of a sudden, in my throat. I wish Em was here. I force myself to sound cheerful. "Great to hear from you, chicken! All the way from the sunny north!"

"You sound suspiciously chipper." I can almost hear Em's narrowed eyes. "Did you and McSpunkNugget get back together?"

"No," I moan glumly. I'm completely out of false sparkle. "He still hates me. But Jed is here and he's cheering me up a bit, even if he is being slightly annoying."

"Jeremy's there? At this time of night."

"In a strictly-platonic-as-always capacity, yes. So what? And oh, by the way, why are you calling me at this unFoldsly hour of the morning, from Noosa?"

"Gold Coast, actually," Em corrects me. "My cousin Peta is having a birthday party, so Mum drove me down for the night. You have no idea how good it is to get away from my insane brother. He's gone into Holiday Hyperdrive, and we have to make all of the sandcastles and do all of the swimming and all of the dancing and *please can I pretend to be a dinosaur one more time* and … gah! It's exhausting! Anyway, so I owe Mum big time for driving me away from the mini maniac. *Plus,* you'll never guess who else is here at the party!"

There's a tap at the sliding door. I look out. Jed is standing there with Beezus, and what appears to be a large patch of vomited spider on his black tee-shirt.

"Em, I'm sorry but I have to go," I apologise. "Beezus spewed on Jed."

"Oh, poor Jed. That's ferrets for ya. Little darlings. I miss Ferretto Rocher so much! But hey, back to—"

Jed holds Beezus up by the neck. His face is murderous.

"Sorry! I have to go. Jed is about to throttle Beezus."

"But, Connie! Wait! It's important! You're going to want to—"

"I'll call you back."

I hang up the phone. It's okay. I know Emily will understand. She has Ferretto. She knows how ferret ownership can spin your life into a strange but beautiful tumble of turmoil.

And I will call her back. Just as soon as I've placated Jed.

"Jed, please don't kill Beezus," I say as I walk outside.

"I'm covered in Beezus-juice," Jed moans. "It smells like the fart of an Abzorbaloff."

I wrinkle my nose. "You're right. You do completely reek. But I warned you not to feed her any more ice-cream"

"I don't think it's spider spew. I think it's something dead. Please tell me you have a tee-shirt I can borrow that doesn't have some lame nineties' band's lame tour details on it?"

I shake my head. "Sorry, cowboy. That's just how my tee-shirt drawer rolls. I'll get you one of Dad's."

"Connie, I don't think one of your dad's accountant button-downs is going to go all that great with my biker boots."

"Beggars covered in ferret spew can't be choosers, Jed," I say. "I'll be back in a minute. Please don't kill Beezus while I'm gone."

I go back inside and up the stairs. I'm going straight to my parents' room, to my Dad's wardrobe, to get the dodgiest of his short-sleeved checkered work shirts for Jed to wear. I can't wait to see the look on his face.

But instead of walking to the end of the hallway, to Mum and Dad's room, I stop at mine.

I don't know why. My bedroom door is open. I just go in.

The advent calendar is still on the floor, ripped and empty.

Viggo's photo is still on my bedside table—him in his best Calvin Klein suit, smiling proudly at the camera, holding his School Dux certificate.

Taken the night I told him I loved him and he didn't say it back.

A book Viggo lent me is beside it—*Politics in Australia, 1901-1939.* I didn't get around to starting it before …

My eyes drift over to my CD collection. Along with my favourite nineties' music there are now classical compilations—Mozart, Wagner, Brahms, Beethoven, Tchaikovski—all bought and listened to, over and over, so I'd know what Viggo was talking about. So I could talk back intelligently about the music he loved. Even though he never managed to like any of mine. But that's okay. I know the music I'm into is nowhere near as worthy as the stuff he's into.

Nothing I like is as good as the stuff Viggo likes.

Nothing I do is as good as what he does.

And without him I'm not as good either.

Now I'm not Viggo MacDuff's girlfriend, I'm not in his light anymore. I'm just in my own boring brown murk.

I'm boring, just like I was before I met him.

I'm worthless.

I'm nothing.

I slide down the wall to my bedroom floor, ripping my favourite Spiderbait poster on the way down. I'd only just blue-tacked it back up.

Viggo hated all the posters on my walls. He thought they made my room look "juvenile".

For the past year, I'd had framed prints on my walls, ones that "toned with the décor of my room". They were grown-up and sensible and *smart*—all the things I'd pretended to be.

But it *was* all pretending. Viggo is gone. "Congo" is gone and I'm back to being stupid, immature, *worthless* Connie again.

Viggo is gone.

Viggo is gone.

Viggo is *gone*.

My chest begins to heave with silent sobs.

I lie down on the carpet, curling my fingers through the shaggy pile and I weep. I weep for a year of being utterly, all-consumingly in love with the best, most clever, most articulate, most *perfect* person I've ever known—a person who made me feel like I was worth something. Like I was the sort of girl someone like that would want to be with.

Like I wasn't a freak.

Like I wasn't the girl the boys thought was one of them, because my best friend is a boy and because I don't wear dresses and heels and listen to Ed Sheeran and squeal like a toddler whenever someone mentions whatever inane YouTuber is flavour of the month.

Like I was worth loving.

Because I know he loved me, even if he never said it in so many words. He must have loved me, to stay with me for a whole year.

He must have loved me to help me so much, with my clothing choices and food and what music I should be listening to. He helped me improve my general knowledge! He loaned me books. He spent *hours* sitting with me, watching political documentaries he'd already seen before. He *must* have loved me, to have done all that.

And he trusted me to do things for him that he didn't trust

anyone else to do. Like research for his speeches, and making his breakfast and taking notes for him in meetings.

He trusted me. He *loved* me.

And I've thrown it all away. Because of one stupid decision and a few stupid words at a party. I just had to do it, didn't I? I just had to wreck everything.

I hit the sides of my head. "I just *had* to—"

"Had to what?"

His voice is gentle.

"Had to what, Connie-girl?"

His hand is soft on my tear-soaked hair.

"Here. Get up. Take this."

He passes me a tissue, from his pocket.

I sniff. "Is it clean?"

I meet his eyes. They are so full of pity. "It's clean, Connie. Blow your nose and give me a hug, okay?"

Through a massive nose-blow that would be embarrassing if I did it in front of anyone but Jed (I shudder at what Viggo would make of it), I say, "Who are you and what have you done with my hard-ass best friend?"

"Shut up and hug me," he grumbles. His cheeks have turned pink. "Don't tell me you don't need one."

"I can't tell you that, because it's not true," I admit. I fall into his arms.

It feels good.

"Are you ready to talk?" he asks. "I'll even ignore the fact you didn't bring me a clean shirt. I found one of your dad's that wasn't too hideous, by the way." He points down at one of Dad's old eighties cricket tee-shirts. It has a picture of Merv Hughes on it.

"Howzat," Jed says.

"That's the least hideous one you could find?" I wrinkle my nose.

Jed shrugs. "It was at the front of the wardrobe. I didn't want to go rifling around. Never know what you'll find at the back of an accountant's cupboard!"

"It's *my dad*," I point out.

Jed grins. "You're right. The worst I would have found is a stack of nineteen-eighty-five *Money* magazines or a talking Boonie doll." His face turns serious. "Do you want to keep doing this, Connie? Talking about Viggo? And the adventures ... We don't even have to start. The spiders were more than enough. We can totes stop there."

I shake my head. "No, I want to. I just had a ... moment. I'll be fine. The next memory is a nice one, anyway."

"Will that make you feel good or bad?"

I sigh. "I don't know. But I think I have to feel it all—good and bad. It might be the only way I can get over him."

"I'll get comfortable then." Jed puts a pillow behind his back and leans on the side of my bed. Then he snaps his fingers. "Oh, wait. We're forgetting something."

Just at that moment, Beezus pushes his way into the room.

Yes, he knows how to open my bedroom door. Ferret MENSA in on speed dial ...

"There's the little champ!" Jed says, smiling.

"You don't hate him?" I ask.

Jed shakes his head. "No. We made up. Besides, I know this little fuzzy, fangy thing is your other best friend, so he should probably be here to hear some of these memories, too."

"You are a very gracious and magnanimous dude," I say. "Pity *your* other best friend isn't so forgiving." I mumble the last part.

"Do you ever think maybe he doesn't have that much to forgive?" Jed says gently.

"You don't know what I did," I protest. I take Beezus from Jed's hands and scratch behind his little ears.

"True. But I know Viggo and I know that he can be a bit ...

finicky. So maybe if you want to tell me what it was that made him mad …"

"No. We're not talking about why Viggo and I broke up. That's the twenty-fifth memory. Now, do you want to hear the fourth one? It has the fifth one tacked on the end too, so it's a two-for-the-price-of-one deal."

"You know me. I'm always a sucker for one of those deals," Jed says. "Do you remember when I got fifteen packets of banana marshmallows, just because there was a 'buy two, get one free' offer on at IGA?"

"I remember," I say, rolling my eyes. "I had to help you eat them when you realised the reason they'd been reduced was that they went out of date the next day. I never want to see another banana marshmallow for the rest of my days. Funnily enough, though, marshmallows feature in this exact Viggo memory."

"Craziness!"

"Insanity!" I laugh. And I realise in that moment how much I've missed hanging out with Jed. I haven't done it enough this past year.

He makes me laugh. Viggo made me feel many things, but he didn't often make me laugh. He's a very serious person. That's why he's such a high achiever.

That, and the fact that he spends most of his waking hours studying, or preparing or just, generally, improving himself.

Which is what he was doing that Friday night, when I turned up on his doorstep.

Wearing another one of Emily's dresses.

TEN

Memory 4

"You look ... well, shall I say, very greatly improved," Viggo said.

I stepped through his front door. My elbow bumped a little on his arm. "Sorry."

"Never mind." He smiled warmly. "I barely felt it. I work out a lot."

I laughed. He didn't. I stopped laughing quickly. What had I done wrong? It was a joke, wasn't it?

But then he smiled again and it was okay. It was better than okay. "You can give it a rub, if you like."

I reached out and tentatively patted Viggo's shirt. It was a nice shirt. It was pale mauve, and made from stiff, perfectly ironed linen. He'd matched it with a darker purple tie, and beige chinos.

He was definitely not dressed for a night in.

So maybe, just maybe ...

Maybe this was actually a date!

I had dared to hope, spurred on by Emily. It seemed ridiculous to me that someone like Viggo would look twice at someone like me.

But maybe ...

"Come in, won't you?" Viggo said, ushering me inside.

I caught him casting a quizzical look at my bag.

"What?" I asked. "I know it doesn't exactly go with the dress—" I was wearing a knee-length pink one this time, with a flouncy skirt. "But it's my favourite. From the markets. Handmade and everything." I showed him the hand-sewn patches with orang-utans and trees on them. "Limited ... edition." My voice dried up as I noticed he didn't look all that impressed.

"Oh, no, it's not the bag itself." Viggo opened one of the hallway doors on to a sitting room filled with books. We walked inside and he motioned for me to take a seat. "Although, it is ... unconventional. I was just thinking it looked rather empty. Where are your books?"

"My ... what?" I sat down on the tasteful black leather couch, a sinking feeling in my belly.

Books? No, I didn't have books in my bag. I had one book—a new Joshua Santospirito graphic novel. I also had my mobile, my Walkman (a joke present from Jed that I actually loved), my sketchpad and pens, a couple of mixed tapes Jed made me to go with the Walkman, and half a packet of Minties.

Because Em had led me to believe there might be kissing.

There is, usually, call for mints on dates. Or so I'd been led to believe.

You didn't usually need books on a date though, did you?

I was really, really, really wishing now that I hadn't spaced out during our phone conversation. I really wanted to know what I was actually doing at Viggo MacDuff's house.

"Your books," Viggo said. "You know, for our study session?"

"Study session!"

Jed is holding his sides, chortling. I whack him on the arm. "Thanks very much for your sympathy and compassion!" I cry. "It was mortifying! Here was I all dressed up in this horrible pink confection of Emily's, and Viggo thought I was there to help him catch up on *Of Mice and Men*."

"And this was before you realised Viggo dresses in a shirt and *tie*—"

"All the time," I finish, wincing. "Except for bed, when he wears—"

"Blue striped pyjamas," we say in unison.

"He has seven pairs." Jed shakes his head. "From Harrods. So is that the end of that memory? It was kind of short."

"I split it into two parts," I explain, stretching my arms over my head. I'm still holding Beeezus and she makes a funny little "eep" noise. "The bad part and the good part."

Jed yawns. "It's, what, one-thirty in the morning? Unless the good part is really freaking good, I'm going to fall asleep right here. Are there zombies or Martian warships or evil, tentacled overlords, or ..."

I laugh and shake my head. "No. They come later. But there is Bach and stinky cheese ..."

"Can I just curl up in your beanbag and catch forty winks?" Jed asks, rubbing his red-rimmed eyes.

"Okay," I say. "I'll just tell this one to Beezus."

ELEVEN

Memory 5

"I was very much hoping to come up to speed with what I've missed in English during the first few months of term," Viggo said, rubbing his perfectly smooth, tanned forehead. "You know, when I was travelling around Europe as part of my prize for winning the Prime Minister's History Awards for my work on the building of the English Houses of Parliament?"

"I know," I said meekly.

"You don't have any of your notes with you?" he asked as he poured me a glass of something whiffy from an expensive-looking bottle.

"I don't, it's true," I said. "I am an idiot." I took the glass even though I'd only ever drunk wine once before, at a dinner party with my parents. It came from a cask and tasted like Beezus's breath.

"Now, Constance." Viggo smiled. "I wasn't chastising you. I was simply pointing out that, as you don't have your notes on you, there's no point framing this as a study session any longer. We should instead simply enjoy one another's company. Play some music, drink a glass of 2012 Moorilla cloth label—only a glass, mind, as we are underage." Viggo *flashed me a grin and I realised this time he was making a joke. I laughed obligingly. Viggo trying to be funny was kind of cute.*

"I've prepared a cheese plate, too. I'll get that soon. I just need to have a think about how we can best confront this change in circumstances."

I looked at my feet, ashamed of myself. "I'm really so sorry," I mumbled. "I can go."

"Oh, you being here is not inconvenient in the slightest. I had nothing scheduled for this time aside from the study session. It's simply inconvenient that I won't have the benefit of your vast experience to assist me attain a level playing field with my scholarly peers. I am behind in all my subjects because of my study trip, and I am doing my best to catch up. And English is … it's the subject I find myself least engaged with."

"Really?" I asked, taking a tiny sip of the wine. It wasn't as bad as I expected. Kind of … smoky. And a bit, almost, flowery. Sort of. With, kind of, cinnamon or something.

"Light, isn't it?" Viggo said. "Fresh and light and …" He sniffed his glass. "Just a hint of blackberry."

"Just what I was thinking," I lied. "Um, but you were saying? About not being great at English? That seems strange, because you speak so well."

"Oh, I can do all the grammar and spelling and punctuation and whatnot." Viggo waved a hand. "It's the creative business, and the analysis of metaphors and similes and that sort of thing. I suppose I prefer things to be more explicit. Factual. I'm not well versed in imagery and I find saying one thing and meaning another … pointless. Just say what you mean. You understand?"

I nodded, even though I didn't agree with Viggo at all. I love poetry and symbolism and playing around with language. I love the beauty of a well-crafted sentence; I admire the skill needed to choose the perfect combination of words. And metaphors and similes and analogies? When they're done well, they are … exciting.

But I nodded. Because I wanted to agree with Viggo. I wanted Viggo to think I wasn't a total idiot.

I wanted Viggo to like me.

And I knew, somehow, that Viggo wouldn't like me so much if I didn't agree with him.

"Anyway, my point is, if we aren't to be studying tonight, we should make the best of a bad situation. Or—" He must have caught the hurt look on my face. "Not bad situation, exactly, because, well, I enjoyed your company the other night at Ronaldo's, so …"

My heart raced.

He enjoyed my company?

That was good, right?

"Thanks, I enjoyed your company too," I said.

"So we can enjoy each other's company again tonight! Tell me, do you like Bach?"

"Um—"

"Don't bother answering." Viggo stood up, smoothing down his already-smooth trousers. "Everybody likes Bach, of course! I'll put some on."

Viggo wandered over to the state-of-the-art sound system in the corner of the room, pressed a few buttons and music filled the room.

He turned, smiling serenely. "Ahh, listen to that," he purred. "I do love this concerto, don't you? Don't answer that. Everyone loves this concerto. Now, Constance, tell me, why do you put those peculiar colours in your hair?"

TWELVE

"He said that?"

"You weren't meant to be listening!" I accused.

"Sorry. Couldn't help myself. My 'Tool Radar' pinged me awake. Viggo really is a complete—"

"No," I interrupt. "He isn't a complete whatever-you're-about-to-say. He just speaks his mind. I respect that. He fights for his right to express his opinion, and he actually has the intelligence to—"

Jed claps his hand over my mouth. "I'm sorry, Princess, but for the time being I'm over hearing about Viggo MacDuff. I think it's time for an adventure. If you really think you can handle it. And, by the by, the only fighting for a right I want to hear about now is …"

"To party!" we sing together.

After I finish giggling, I say seriously, "We're not actually going to party, are we? Because I'm not really dressed for it."

Jed looks at me enigmatically. "We can't party. We don't have any bananas!"

"'Always take a banana to a party, Rose. Bananas are good!'" I quote. "Tenth doctor, to Rose Tyler. 'Girl in the Fireplace' episode. So where *are* we going then, Jed, in our banana-less state?"

"We, Connie-girl, are off to find a twenty-four-hour chemist."

"Dare I ask?"

Jed stands and takes my hand. "You may ask, Connie-girl, but that would spoil the element of surprise. And you know …"

Jed pulls me up and I'm now standing eye-to-eye with him.

There's a tiny, inexplicable twitch in my belly.

I ignore it.

Jed leans in and whispers in my ear. His breath is warm. "Nobody expects—"

"If you're going to say 'The Spanish Inquisition'—"

"I was going to say 'an army of evil shop dummies'. But yeah, those Spanish dudes too."

"I expect the Spanish dudes," I say, pulling back slightly. "But then, I am an 'expect-the-worst' kind of girl."

"You never used to be," Jed says sadly. "Before you met Viggo MacDuff."

THIRTEEN

My hair is blue.

Bright, Cookie Monster blue. And not just streaked with it, either—I've done that before. All of it is blue, from the roots to the tips. Every strand.

Blue.

I look like a Muppet has crawled on to my head and died.

"Viggo will hate it," I moan. "He'll never get back together with me with my hair like this."

"And we care … why?"

Jed passes me a chip. We're sitting on my front step. I have a towel wrapped around my shoulders and we're letting my hair dry in the cool night air. Jed has cooked bake-in-the-oven fries for breakfast.

At three am.

Apparently the walk to the chemist made him hungry. And I'm not complaining. I'm in the mood for some serious comfort eating. "Why are you being so mean about Viggo now?" I ask. "He's meant to be your best friend. You were on his side earlier."

"I was never on his side. I did think maybe there was a tiny chance you'd actually done something not completely awesome to make him leave you—"

"I *did*," I protest.

Jed shakes his head. "Sounds like, whatever you did, Viggo deserved it. And besides, he's actually not all that—"

"Arrrgghh!" I cry. "How many times do I have to tell you? I don't want *you* to talk about Viggo!"

"Why?" Jed raps me on the head with an especially long chip. "Why won't you let me talk about Viggo? Why won't you let me tell you—"

"Because you already told me he doesn't want to get back together with me," I mumble. "That was bad enough. I don't want to know any more. It hurts too much."

"Talking about the memories isn't hurting enough?" Jed asks softly.

I shake my head. "They were good times. Hopeful times. In-love times. While I tell you about those times, I get caught up in what I'm saying and I can sort of relive it and pretend ... that *now* isn't happening. You were right, Jed—saying this stuff out loud is helping me. But you telling me how *Viggo* is *now*—especially how he doesn't want to be with me and how angry he must be at me —that doesn't help."

"But what if I told you—"

"No."

The word silences Jed. He stuffs a handful of chips in his mouth. While he's chewing, I take the opportunity. "I'm going to tell you another memory now," I say. "Okay?"

Jed nods. "Mkerr," he says through a mouthful of chips.

"Okay, so, where did I get up to?"

FOURTEEN

Memory 6

I left Viggo's house after about an hour. Viggo was in the middle of an epically comprehensive explanation of quantum physics when he looked at his watch and announced that, as it was nearly six-thirty, he had to go and cook dinner for his family.

"You cook dinner?" I asked. "What, every night?"

He lifted a shoulder. "Unless I have a meeting or event to appear at. I like it. I make a point of attending classes with the best international chefs when I travel overseas. Most of the world's top chefs are male, you know. Not that I intend to become a chef, but it might impress at dinner parties, with foreign dignitaries or the like."

"Wow. Just ... wow," I breathed. I felt as if I was having heart palpitations.

And I know—I know—I'd transformed in the space of a week from Connie Chase, nerdy tomboy to Constance Chase, character from a Bad Regency Novel, the sort of person who would have completely bemused the old Connie, but ...

He could cook. And he was smart. And he talked to me like I was smart too.

And he could cook.

I couldn't cook to save myself. Apart from bake-in-the-oven chips and microwave waffles. And I couldn't sew, though I was a demon with a bedazzler and a badge press.

"I could teach you," Viggo said, as if reading my mind.

"To cook?"

"And to sew. You could mend my shirts for me."

If anybody else had said that exact thing, it would have sounded so misogynist, but the way Viggo said it, with a twinkle in his eye and a wry smile … it was sexy. In a retro, American TV sitcom husband kind of way.

"I'm joking, of course," he went on, though. "There is nothing worse than the look of a darned shirt. I just ask Catherine to order a new one when one of mine tears."

"Do your shirts often tear?" I asked.

Viggo just raised an eyebrow and smirked at me. If I hadn't known any better, I would have said that the look on his face was … almost flirtatious.

But then he clapped his hands. "Well, sorry to shoo you off, but I really must get cracking on dinner. I would invite you to stay, but I don't have enough ingredients this time, and I only have a very humble dish of ratatouille planned. Peasant food. Definitely not salubrious enough for an elegant young woman such as yourself."

I couldn't answer. I just gulped and stood gawping like a goldfish. Me? Elegant? Was I actually living a dream?

That night, I barely slept.

I couldn't stop thinking about Viggo.

I knew I had as much chance of him actually liking me as Amy Pond had against the Weeping Angels (Spoiler alert: zero and zilch), but still …

It was nice to dream. Nice to think someone like Viggo MacDuff might actually like someone like me. Nice to imagine I could be …

Better.

FIFTEEN

Memory 7

The next day at school, after a sleep that felt more like a blink, I looked and felt a wreck. So of course the first person I saw as I stumbled along the corridor—dressed in my lamest old Barenaked Ladies tee-shirt and ripped jeans, extra-large mocha in one hand and packet of Cheezels in the other—was none other than Sir Twinkle-Eyes himself.

He was leaning against my locker, holding a shiny black paper bag with ribbons for handles. "Well, good morning," he said. He looked me up and down. "Interesting outfit."

I mumbled something about running late. It was all I could do not to cry. If I'd had any chance with Viggo before, I definitely didn't now.

"Well, don't feel too bad," Viggo said. "Because I may just have saved your sartorial bacon." He handed over the bag.

"What is it?" I asked.

He nodded at my hands. "Look."

I wiped Cheezel dust on my jeans and reached inside. I felt fabric between my fingers. I pulled out a crisp white shirt. I held it up. It was beautiful. It felt like linen, or really expensive cotton.

"I guessed the size. I'm assuming I did well?"

I nodded in reply, thinking, what sort of guy is able to guess a girl's dress size?

"There's more," Viggo said, smiling.

I reached in again and pulled out a navy skirt—definitely linen—and a matching navy scarf.

"What is all this?" I whispered.

Viggo shrugged. "My sister was having a clean out, following a new health regime that has seen her drop two dress sizes. She was going to send these to a charity shop, but I rescued them. I thought they'd be just perfect for you."

"Wow," I breathed. "But they're so …" I looked at the label again. Yves Saint Laurent. Even I had heard of him. "Snazzy," I finished. "And I'm not sure they're exactly… me." I gestured down at my clothes. "I'm more a jeans-and-tee-shirt kind of girl. You know? I'd look silly in those fancy things."

Viggo shook his head. He stepped closer. "I think you're selling yourself short, Constance Chase. I think you'll look marvellous in these clothes. You are an intelligent, elegant, worldly young woman, capable of great things. And yet you dress like a teenager."

"I am a teenager," I protested.

Viggo laughed. "Well, yes. But you know what I mean."

I didn't. Not really. But I smiled and nodded anyway.

"Will you wear the clothes?" Viggo asked. "For me? And for yourself. You deserve nice things, Constance."

"Um …"

Viggo smiled. "I'll take that as a 'yes'. Now …" He looked at his watch. "You have five minutes before class begins. That's more than enough time to get changed. Would you like me to hold your coffee? Oh, and by the way." He pulled out another parcel. "A new bag. One that is less … homemade. It's Louis Vuitton. You may thank me later by finally showing me those Steinbeck notes of yours. Well, what are you waiting for? Go!"

And so I went into the girl's loos looking like Connie, Nerdfighter, nineties' indie music fan, general geek-about-town, and emerged looking like …

"An air stewardess," Jed grumbles. He raises an eyebrow. "What? I remember that day. I came looking for you at recess and I wouldn't have recognised you at all if it wasn't for your trademark awesome hair." He sighs. "Not that your awesome hair lasted much longer either." He reaches over and twirls a strand of my newly-sapphire locks between his fingers. "I'm glad it's back." He nods at my satchel. "And your not-Louis-Vuitton bag."

"The überclones liked my outfit," I point out. "When I came out of the toilets, Kacey and Karen were in the hallway and Kacey raised an eyebrow and asked 'who' I was wearing. I didn't understand the question. I said Viggo bought them for me. She laughed and said, 'You look good.'"

"And since when did you care about Kacey's Kuusela's opinion? You look good *now*."

"I look like a teenager again," I mumble. "After it happened … after we broke up, I dressed *properly* for, like, an hour. But it felt like I was pretending. Like I was pretending Viggo and I might still have a chance."

"And pretending to be someone you're not. Someone you never were," says Jed.

"I could have been that person!" I argue. "Smart and worldly and stuff. *Elegant.* I *was* that person, when I was with Viggo. You are so down on him for some bizarre reason, but you have no idea how incredible it was being his girlfriend. It was like a whole other world."

"You changed long before you became his girlfriend, though," Jed's voice is flat. "I mean when did you turn into the stewardess? It was, like, August? September? And you two didn't get together until December."

"I had to prove myself," I mumble. "I had to show him I was good enough."

"You sound like an idiot," Jed snaps. "You're not an idiot, Connie. You're smart."

I shake my head. "Viggo is smart. Patience is smart. *I* am an idiot."

Jed lets out a noise like an angry bear. He stands up abruptly. "I'm sick of this," he says. "Time for adventure. Let's get out of here."

"Where are we going?" I ask, following him down the garden path.

"I'd say 'shut up and follow me'," Jed says. "But then I'd sound too much like Viggo MacDuff.

SIXTEEN

"How much further?"

"How many more times are you going to ask me that, Connie? Bangarra isn't that big."

"I feel like I've walked to Smithton."

"Yep. That's it. I've taken you to Smithton. Here we are at Dismal Swamp …"

"Seriously, Jed. How—"

My phone buzzes. I snatch it from my pocket.

Jed groans. "Viggo? Don't reply."

"It's from Em!" I protest, showing him my screen. "Oh, Ben Folds. I was meant to call her back."

"Oh. Sorry. You can look at your phone if you want. Call Em. It's fine. I don't want to tell you what to do, Connie. You've had enough of that."

"Can we make a pact to stop saying bad things about Viggo?" I ask. "Seriously. He's your best friend. And seriously, Jed. You're really getting on my goat."

There's a pause, in which I glower at Jed and he glares back at me. Then one corner of his mouth twitches. "Getting on your goat? Who *says* that? Oh no, wait. Let me guess. Does his name rhyme with Figgo FacFluff?"

I shrug. "I guess I picked it up."

Jed takes my hand. "Connie, I'm sorry if my badmouthing Viggo has upset you. Okay? I promise to stop. If you get your skates on right now."

"I'm sorry," I say. "I *am* hurrying."

"No, I didn't mean it metaphorically," Jed says, shaking his head. He points at the nondescript brick building in front of us. "I mean literally. We're here."

I peer through the dark four am light at the sign on the building. "Bangarra Skaterama? Jed, you know I love me a rollerblade as much as the next nineties' nerd, but it's the middle of the night-slash-un-Ben-Foldsly-morning. How are we going to get in there?"

"So you know my sister, Margrete?"

"Vaguely," I say sarcastically. I've known Meg for as long as I've known Jed. So, like, forever.

"Just got a job here," Jed says.

"And what, you stole her key?"

Jed does a little bounce and produces a square of plastic from his front pocket. "Keypass. Yes. Or, rather, I borrowed it. She owed me a favour or ten."

"And you just knew we were going to go skating tonight?" I ask incredulously.

He shrugs. "I thought it was a possibility ..."

I watch as Jed walks towards the door of the skating rink. He has a nice walk—I've always thought that. Sort of slow and loping and careless. Viggo always walks with *purpose*. He walks as if he was on his way somewhere *important*. Which he usually is.

Jed walks for the sake of walking.

Jed does a lot of things for the sake of doing them. He sits in his backyard for hours, watching the birds. He wanders around parks, rubbing leaves between his fingers, picking up sticks and bending them, swatting at the grass. He finds smooth stones and rolls them in his palm. He gets in Tallulah—when she's functioning—and just drives. Not to anywhere in particular. Wherever the roads take him. He sits for whole mornings, playing with Beezus, smoothing out the velvety fur on her belly, scratching behind her ears. He could spend all day just *being* with her.

And his music ...

Some of the songs he listens to are twenty minutes long. Whenever Jed would put one of them on, Viggo would curl his lip and say, "Is this another ten-hour-long epic about druids and robots? Because, if so, I have somewhere I have to be."

Jed is slow, while Viggo is brisk.

Viggo is excitement and energy. Jed is—despite his love of thumping, racing, pounding, galloping music—calm.

Laid back.

Comfortable.

I feel comfortable with Jed in a way I never felt with Viggo.

But then, what I liked—loved—about Viggo was that he pushed me out of my comfort zone. He challenged me to be *better*. He wanted me to improve myself.

Jed is satisfied with me just as I am. I'd never better myself if Jed and I were ...

I shake myself. If Jed and I were *what?* What in the actual Jabba The Hutt am I thinking about Jed and I being *anything* for?

Anything other than best friends, that is.

I am way overtired, obviously.

But he does have a nice walk.

And I'd forgotten how much I like his hair. It may be Vikingly long, but it's always super clean and shiny and sleek like a horse's mane.

Sometimes, when we sat together on the couch at his house or mine, I'd curl up beside him and run my fingers through his hair, untangling knots and enjoying the satin-ribbon smoothness between my fingers.

Sometimes, I'd annoy him by weaving it into little, girlish braids that made his hair kink and frizz when he unwove them.

I smile at the memory.

I've missed doing that. We haven't hung out together—just the two of us, lazy and slothful and content—for months.

Since Viggo MacDuff arrived.

We haven't gone bowling, either, or to the park for a picnic of pizza and chips.

Or skating.

We used to come here all the time—during less vampish hours. He'd hold my hand and guide me around the rink, challenging me to speed skate and egging me on to try jumping. I could never do it, no matter how many times I tried. But I always tried.

Now, I'm not sure if I should even put the skates on.

What if I fall? What if I hit my nose or get a black eye? What if I break my wrist?

I am already wearing Vans. I already have blue hair. That's probably enough to guarantee that Viggo will never look twice at me again, but if I am all bruised and beaten up, he never will, for sure. He always sneered at tomboy girls with ruddy skin and grazes on their knees. He thought they looked "unladylike" and … uncouth.

No.

No, I haven't skated for so long. I'm out of practice. I could fall just doing normal skating, let alone jumps or turns or …

"Jed," I call out. "Um, I'm not sure I should—"

"And we're in!" he calls out. He turns around and performs an elaborate bow. "The only thanks I expect is for you to share a packet of breakfast Cheezels with me when we're done. And maybe you could do one or two highly dangerous jumps."

"Yeah, about that …" I'm all ready to turn on my scuffed rubber heel and walk away. I mean, breaking into a skating rink in the early hours of Boxing Day morning? Doing jumps when I haven't skated for over a year?

Madness.

Or, as Viggo would say, "Not at all sensible."

But then Jed holds out a hand, and the look on his face …

He's so excited. And whenever Jed is excited about something, I can't help getting excited too. It's infectious. I take his hand and let him lead me from the dawning light into the darkness inside.

"Might have been an idea to ask Meg where the light switches are," I suggest.

"We could just go skating in the dark?" Jed begins humming. It takes me a while to recognise the song.

I laugh. "Can't start a fire without a spark!" I sing. "You are such a dodgy metal fan, quoting Bruce Springsteen."

"You are a dodgy nineties' indie music fan. You knew exactly what I was talking about. We can suck together, hey? You and me, kid. We're, like, in total harmony."

"Like ebony … and ivory!" I sing.

"Yeah, now that's just going too far. Springsteen I can handle. Stevie Wonder and Paul McCartney?" Jed shudders. "Although, *CMJ* did say *Blackwater Park* was a 'metal fusion of Pink Floyd and The Beatles', and it's hands down my favourite Opeth album. Although, you know, in comparison it's definitely more Lennon Beatles than McCart—"

I have to interrupt. Jed on metal can last for hours.

"Hey, Opeth! That leads in nicely to my next memory."

Jed nods. "Tell me while I find these damned light switches."

We're still wandering around in total blackness. I can hear Jed, walking ahead not far away. I creep towards the noise of his footsteps.

Suddenly they stop, but my feet take longer to process this information than my brain does. I keep walking and smack straight into Jed's back.

"Whoa there, Connie-girl," Jed says, reaching out to catch me before I fall backwards.

For a moment we stand, his arms around my waist, breathing together in the darkness.

It feels nice, being held by Jed.

Comfortable.

Safe.

"Hey," he says softly.

"Hey," I reply.

I reach up and I can feel Jed's smooth hair beneath my hands. He's breathing heavily and I realise I am too.

What is going on here?

Just then, something between Jed and me vibrates. At first I think it's some sort of electricity between us, some sort of charge …

But then I realise it's a phone. Jed's phone. It's flashing in his pocket.

"You should get that," I whisper.

"It's just a message," he says. The phone has lit up his face from below, illuminating it in parts, but leaving others in shadow. His eyes are glimmering. His eyelashes look even darker and longer in silhouette.

My stomach lurches.

What in the *actual* …

"Shouldn't you check it?" I ask, pulling away from him. "I mean, it might be important."

"Do you want me to check it?" Jed asks and I hear a note of hurt in his voice. But that can't be right, can it? Jed doesn't get hurt. Jed's tough. He's *metal*. He doesn't get hurt feelings. Especially not by me.

"Yeah, go for it," I say. "I'll use my phone light to see if I can find the switches. Don't know why we didn't think of it before."

"Ood-heads," Jed says, and the playful tone is back in his voice. I'm relieved. I like this Jed better.

I *know* this Jed.

I'm comfortable with this Jed.

I move slowly around the perimeter of the room, hand on the wall, holding up my phone and checking for switch boxes.

Finally, after a minute or two, I find them and push. The room bursts into light.

I look around to find Jed. He's still staring at his phone, a cheerful expression on his face.

"Let there be light!" I announce. He doesn't look up. "What? Who's the message from?"

"Nobody," he says, too quickly. The smile drops.

"Ooh! Nobody!" I tease. "Is it, perchance, a *female nobody?*"

Jed looks back up and that face is there again.

"I'll take that as a 'yes'," I say lightly. "Do I know this person?"

"Actually, you do," Jed says, a hint of snappish in his tone. "Leah McKenzie."

"Leah?" I wrack my brain. The name does sound familiar … And then I remember. "She was at the party. Grade eleven girl? Why is she texting you?" My mouth drops open. "Jed, you *didn't* …"

Jed flashes a half-grin. "Neither confirming nor denying. Until we get to that particular memory. I assume you included a memory of the party in your twenty-five?"

I nod, trying to ignore the empty feeling in my gut. *Neither confirming or denying …*

Why do those words make my belly twist?

"Then, when we get to the party, I'll tell you about Leah Mackenzie. But first, we need to skate." Jed points at the row of inline skates and conventional ones behind the counter across the room. "And, as we skate, you will tell me the next memory. I believe it involves a certain Swedish melodic death metal band?"

"Oh yeah," I reply. I shake myself. I'm being an idiot. After all, why should I care if Jed hooked up at the party? He's done it before. He'll do it again. Why tonight—or this early morning—do I care?

I don't. That's the answer. I'm just overtired.

"Let's get our skates on," I say breezily. "And I'll tell you about Opeth."

SEVENTEEN

"You were there for this memory."

"I figured I must be," Jed says. "Considering it involves Opeth."

"There are actually a couple of memories bundled up in this one, though. Some involve fashion."

"I can handle it."

"Good. Right. So, it was November. We were all starting to prepare for final exams."

Jed laughs. "Some of us more than others."

I elbow him in the ribs. He almost drops the skate he's holding by its laces. "Oi!" He elbows me back. "Go on then."

I finish tying my own skate laces in a double bow (just to be safe). "All right. So it was November and Viggo had invited me over to his house for an 'intensive study session'."

"I *do* know this one!"

"Jed?"

"Yup?"

"Shush."

Jed mimes zipping his lips.

I close my eyes. And remember. "I'd just done something pretty drastic in preparation for this night." I peer at my best friend, who nods mutely. "Yep," I say. "I thought you'd remember this."

EIGHTEEN

Memory 8

Viggo hated the colours in my hair.

He told me how much more sophisticated I'd look if they were gone; how people would take me more seriously; how the teachers at school might even consider me for more prizes and awards if they thought I was "more committed to my education".

"And you think they'll think that if I get rid of the streaks?"

Viggo nodded. "Definitely," he said. "The way you choose to present yourself has an enormous impact on people's perception of you and your capabilities and priorities. If you chose to present yourself more ... elegantly, the teachers might consider it more feasible to place their faith in you. They would consider you more reliable. They would feel less as if they'd be played for fools by investing in your education and future."

I nodded. I did love my Paintbox highlights, but—

It might be nice to win an award. Or two. For something other than art or English.

I could be someone who won prizes.

I could be someone like Viggo.

Would it only take dyeing my hair brown to clinch it?
If so, it was worth a try, wasn't it?
"I'll do it," I promised him. "I'll make myself look sophisticated."
Viggo's mouth lifted at a corner. "I knew you would," he said.

NINETEEN

Memory 9

"Are you sure?" Em asked, dye brush hovering over my freshly-washed hair. Two hyperactive ferrets wrestled at our feet. "I mean, it's not … you, Connie. It's so … brown. So basic."

"It's the new me," I declared. "I'm growing up, Em. That's not basic. That's life."

"That's sad," she said.

"Not everyone can be The Doctor," I replied. "Not everyone can stay young forever."

"A) I never know what you're talking about when you mention 'The Doctor'," she said. "And b) you can stay young forever. I intend to. Jed intends to. It's all in your attitude."

"Well, I have a new attitude." I pulled Beezus to my chest and gave him a last nuzzle as a pink-haired person. "And it's all about being elegant. And mature."

"How very, very dull, bae," Em said. But she shrugged and plopped a dollop of brown goop right on top of my head …

TWENTY

Memory 10

And then, the next day, I bought a new dress. All by myself, from Country Road.

I had never shopped in Country Road before. I'd never really shopped anywhere other than the Salvos and the vintage racks at Salamanca. The only new clothes I had were the ones Mum bought me and they mostly came from Target.

I had no idea how to do Country Road. It was like another planet.

I thanked the heavens there were natives available to help, otherwise I might never have made it out alive.

"Can I help you, hun?" the sales assistant asked, straightening the collar of her burnt orange tunic.

I panicked. "That one you're wearing? The dress thing? Is it from here?"

"Of course, hun. Staff discount!" Bella laughed. "But seriously, this would look beyond cute on you. Go get undressed. I'll find your size."

As I walked out into Centrepoint, I noticed Kacey Kuusela standing behind the counter of a different boutique. Another one I'd never have been *seen dead in pre-Viggo. She lifted her head just as I passed and gave me a wave and a sunny smile.*

The world had literally turned upside down.

I smiled back nervously, and she mimed yawning. "Come in?" she beckoned with a hand. I shook my head apologetically and pointed at my watch. She shrugged and mouthed, "Next time."

The world had literally turned upside-down and inside-out and been turned into an Asylum for the Daleks.

I ran a hand through my newly all-brown hair. Maybe that had something to do with why Kacey was being so nice. Because I looked normal now.

I just hoped Viggo liked me this way.

TWENTY-ONE

Memory 11

On the bus, on the way home to complete the final part of my transformation, Viggo was all I could think of.

I wanted Viggo to approve of the new me. I wanted Viggo to like me.

Love me.

My little crush was something much deeper now.

It was as if some other girl had inhabited my body: a girl who hadn't always been a nerdy tomboy, who hadn't spent the better part of her life being best friends with a boy for whom fashion is whichever black shirt smells least like armpit. A girl who hadn't ditched her Grade Ten leaver's dinner because there was a Doctor Who special on, who hadn't spent a year's savings on tickets to Ben Folds with the Tasmanian Symphony Orchestra.

I knew it was bizarre. I knew I was acting so out-of-character everyone must be thinking I was possessed, but it was as if Viggo had cast a powerful spell on me. He made me feel I could be better; I could be worth something. I could be the "best version of myself", as Viggo himself would put it.

He opened my eyes.

He made me realise there was more than mooching around with Jed, *coming up with harebrained schemes. There was more than wasting all my time on some new nerdy obsession. There was more than skiving off class to go to CD shops, or spending whole weekends watching nineties' video clips on YouTube, or brainstorming ideas with Jed for my next superhero graphic novel.*

There was more to life.

More to me.

I'm pretty sure my parents thought I was on drugs. I kept catching them looking at me anxiously over the dinner table when they saw I was reading Proust instead of Gaiman; when I watched political documentaries instead of Doctor Who or Red Dwarf; when I told them I was going to study at Viggo's instead of to Wong's with Jed.

And Patience gently asked if I'd joined a cult.

But I didn't care.

I liked the new "me".

And the new me wore burnt orange dresses with peplums on the hips. The new me had all-brown hair. The new me might even ... wear a hint of makeup?

As I got off the bus, I ran my hand over my makeup-free face, trying to imagine what I'd look like when I walked back out of the house in an hour or so ...

TWENTY-TWO

Memory 12

The world had been turned upside-down and inside-out and turned into an Asylum for Daleks presided over by mad Missy and all stuffed inside a Tardis full of dinosaurs.

Or, in Layman's terms, things were going a bit cuckoo in my world.

I didn't even own any makeup.

Thankfully, Patience had a tonne of free-with-magazine face-stuff stored in our shared bathroom cabinet, just ripe for sneaky pilfering by love-struck big sisters.

Or, I should say, I would have been able to sneakily pilfer the makeup, had I known what half of it was for.

I had to ask Patience for help.

"Contouring is what the Kardashians do," she explained, rolling her eyes when it was obvious I had no idea who or what a Kardashian was. "It's kind of like shading your face," she said. That I understood.

That was art.

"Okay. So, like, covering up the bad bits with shadow and making the good bits ... brighter?"

"Kinda. I'll show you. Priming is first, though. It's like the undercoat you use when painting your house. Make sense?"

"I don't want my face to look like a wall!" I cried. "I might just, um, try these." I held out some browny-pink lipstick and a clear mascara.

"Aww, you're no fun," Patience teased as she carefully swiped the mascara wand over my eyelashes, biting her lower lip in concentration.

"But am I beautiful, Mon cheri?" I asked in a poor attempt at a French accent.

"You were before," Patience said softly. "You don't need makeup to be beautiful."

Did I mention I adore my little sister?

"Is this for a boy?" she asked shyly. Patience is just at the age where boys have only just made the transition from "icky" to "cute", and she blushed as she spoke.

"Maybe," I said, feeling every bit as bashful as my twelve-year-old sister.

"He better be really good," Patience said. "Because you deserve good."

"He's the best."

Patience grinned. "Excellent," she said. "Because if he isn't, he'll have me to deal with."

"Oh yeah? What are you going to do? 'Nice' him to death?"

Patience's eyes narrowed. "Do not underestimate me, sisterino," she said gravely. Then she smirked again. "Right. Done. Do you like it?"

I swivelled towards the mirror and my throat tightened.

I saw the person in the mirror wrinkle her brow. Then touch her face tentatively. I looked at the fingers. They looked just like mine. But the rest …

It was me. But it wasn't.

The person in the mirror looked …

Like an überclone.

I wanted to hate it. The old Connie would have hated it. But Constance … kind of liked it.

I just hoped Viggo would too.

TWENTY-THREE

Memory 13

I turned up on his doorstep at precisely five pm.

Viggo appreciated—no, expected—punctuality. I'd learned this the hard way on the sole occasion when I'd been late for one of our now-weekly study sessions. His face remained impassive as ever, but he did say, pointedly, "Oh, hello, Constance. I'd assumed you weren't coming. I thought we'd agreed on five pm?"

It was seven minutes past five.

I knew now to be on time and I also knew to ring the doorbell (knocking is "uncouth"), and only once, and then wait patiently for Viggo to answer, which he always did within thirty seconds of my ringing.

I'd timed it.

Except, this day, Viggo didn't answer the doorbell.

And I heard, instead of Brahms or Beethoven wafting serenely up the hallway towards me, the familiar thumping of an Opeth CD.

"Have I come to the wrong house?" I asked, suppressing my disappointment. Why was Jed there? This was my time with Viggo!

"Have I opened the door to the wrong person?" Jed asked, his eyes boggling. "Seriously, what have you done with my best friend?"

"You like it?" I asked, twirling.

"I do." I looked behind Jed. Viggo was coming down the stairs.

And he was looking at me … differently.

He was looking at me as if he really did like what he saw.

TWENTY-FOUR

"And that's it?" Jed asks. He's stopped skating and is facing me, a grimace twisting his face. "Seriously, I get ten minutes of 'I was wearing this' and 'my hair was like this' and 'Ooh, I wore mascara' and then, boom, Viggo *looks at you*. And that's the end of the memory? Or, like, five memories, or however many pointless mini-memories you bundled into one?"

"It was a meaningful look," I call over my shoulder as I skate past him. "Our first meaningful look."

"And there was I standing there and not even noticing." Jed catches up to me. "I was too busy gawping at your boring hair and hideous dress."

"And forcing Viggo to listen to Opeth."

Jed grins wickedly. "I'd forgotten about that. He lost a bet."

"Viggo lost a bet?" Now *my* eyes are boggling. I can't imagine Viggo MacDuff losing *anything*.

Jed raises an eyebrow. He's skating backwards in front of me now.

I hate how he can do that.

"You didn't wonder why Opeth was playing in the immaculate MacDuff residence?"

"Um …" To tell the truth, I hadn't really thought much about it. I'd been too busy thinking about Viggo's face; the way his eyes were caressing me, taking in my body in a way that wasn't lascivious or sleazy but still expressed his … enjoyment. When Viggo looked at me, everything else melted away, even Mikael Akerfeldt's devilish growl. "What was the bet?"

Jed grimaces. "He bet me I couldn't carry a piano across the room all by myself."

"Right. And why would he bet you that?"

Jed's face darkens. "I can only assume because he needed a piano moved across a room and he couldn't be bothered doing it himself, and I was getting tired of being his slave just for the sake of it, so he came up with an evil plan to manipulate me into doing it some other way."

"Viggo wouldn't do that!" I cry.

"*Sure* he wouldn't." Jed rolls his eyes. "Whatever. Just tell me the next memory is even a wafer more exciting than those ones? Otherwise I may have to deliberately skate into that wall and concuss myself. Hospitalisation would be far preferable to 'Oh, and, by the way, I wore pinky-brown lipstick'." He imitates my voice and then mimes vomiting.

"It is," I say smugly. "I jump forward a bit in the next memory."

"To when?"

"To my birthday."

"*The* birthday?" Jed looks interested now. He stops skating again and sits down, right there in the middle of the rink. "Stop everything," he says. "Tell me. Now."

TWENTY-FIVE

Memory 14

Patience was born on Valentine's Day and I blasted into the world two days before Christmas. That's why Mum and Dad make a special effort every year to throw us a truly great party. So we don't feel as though our birthdays are being hijacked by other holidays.

So we feel important.

When I was little, the parties were your typical kid event - fruit kebabs and fairy bread and koala cakes from the Women's Weekly cookbook; pin-the-tail-on-the-donkey and Twister and duck, duck, goose.

As I grew older (though, sadly, no cooler), I asked for Dungeons and Dragons parties, or Star Wars ones, or we all dressed up as wizards and knights and acted out mediaeval warfare in our backyard. And then every second year I had a Doctor Who party, and dressed as a different doctor each time.

Yep, I was always that awesome.

It was at one of my parties that I first met Jed.

We were in Grade Five. My party that year had a "Pokemon" theme. It was back when Pokemon was enjoying a brief moment of coolness and, even *though I was feeling mildly disgruntled about that—after all, I liked it way before everyone else had caught on—I was thrilled that my classmates were excited about my party, and that every one of them had RSVP-ed yes.*

One of my classmates, Kyron, asked me the day before the party if he could bring his neighbour along.

"Mum wants us to be friends," he said wearily. "She's been trying to get us to hang out for, like, months, because his best friend went off to the jungle or something and he's gone all emo and Mum reckons he's sad and I should, like, save him or whatever. I'm meant to be playing with him on Saturday but, you know, you're doing Pokemon so of course I have to come, but Mum said I can only come if he comes, so—"

"Does he like Pokemon?" I asked, narrowing my eyes.

Kyron nodded. "And Doctor Who. And music."

Everyone at my school knew I loved Doctor Who. And that I was a music nerd. While they were all listening to Beyonce and Rihanna, on my iPod I had Nirvana and Regurgitator. And, of course, Whatever and Ever Amen (still the best Ben Folds album of all time). When they wore surf brand tee-shirts to school, I wore my band ones. While they collected nail stickers, I collected vintage vinyl LPs.

I know it might sound like I was edgy—the sort of kid every other kid at school would want to be friends with—but this was not the case. When you're ten, anything different is not intriguing or tempting, it's weird and scary.

The only reason I always had lots of people at my birthday parties (even when I wasn't doing Pokemon), was because my parties were known for being so awesome the kids could get past their mistrust and wariness of oddball Connie for a couple of hours of party fun.

I knew the other kids didn't really like me. And I wish I could say it didn't bother me, but it did. I wanted to be liked. By even one person.

So when Kyron asked if he could bring a friend, one who liked Doctor Who and music and was lonely, just like me, of course I said yes.

And even though he was into Metallica and not Modest Mouse, we knew at first sight we were soul mates. We were both weirdos; both passionate about the nerdy things we loved. I knew within seconds we'd be best friends for life and that he'd be there at every other birthday party I ever had.

By the next year, he was not only attending the parties, he was helping me organise them.

TWENTY-SIX

Memory 15

It was his idea that my sweet sixteenth should have a "nineties' bubble-gum pop" theme.

"What? It's ironic," he said. "Everyone knows you're into the serious and worthy nineties' music, not Aqua and Westlife. They'll know you're doing it tongue-in-cheek. Don't worry. Your cred will remain intact." He looked at me suspiciously. "You do still like nineties' music, don't you, Connie-girl? Or has my Other Best Friend completely Stepford-Wifed you into submission and a penchant for Baroque string quartets?"

I looked down at my fingernails. They were French manicured. Viggo's sister Catherine had invited me along to her "nail therapy" appointment. Of course, it would have been rude to say no. And Viggo encouraged me to go. He said his sister could use some "girl time", and, just as an aside, he mentioned that he loves the look of French manicures.

But that wasn't why I picked the neutral nails instead of the black glitter ones that had looked kind of cool, too.

The black ones were sure to chip within hours and then it would be a waste of money, wouldn't it? Whereas, if I did mess up the nearly nude polish, it would be less noticeable. It really had nothing to do with Viggo's preferences and all to do with practicality.

It didn't make me a Stepford Wife. Neither did my new Ted Baker dress pants. They were an investment. I could wear them to my art tutoring lessons and to school, and because they were expensive (even though I did get them on sale), they were sure to last lots longer than the old black skinny leg jeans I used to wear before.

At least, that's what Kacey Kuusela told me when she sold them to me.

Yes, I know, I bought clothing from one of the überclones but, actually, she was quite nice to me when Em and I went into the boutique where she worked.

In fact, she'd been quite nice to me ever since Viggo arrived and I started dressing a bit more, well, "basic" and acting a bit less ... weird. The wave-and-smile in the mall that day wasn't a one-off. Kacey Kuusela actually seemed to like me.

She was so nice to me on the day I bought the pants, in fact, that Em said, "See, I told you that you'd get along if you just gave her a chance."

"She's still an überclone," I protested half-heartedly.

"What does that even mean?" asked Em.

"You know, she and her friends: they all talk the same, look the same, dress the same ..."

"Hmm ..." Em looked thoughtful. "I wonder if they all dress in clothes from that shop." She looked pointedly at the carrier bags I held in my hands.

But it wasn't true. I wasn't turning into an überclone. I wasn't a replica. I wasn't a Stepford Wife.

"Of course I still like nineties' music," I told Jed defiantly. "Nineties' bubble-gum pop party it is. It will be awesome."

Jed looked happier than I'd seen him in months.

TWENTY-SEVEN

Memory 16

Of course, the awesomeness of Jed's party idea seemed much less when I answered the door to Viggo MacDuff, dressed as Baby Spice.

Jed dared me.

It seemed like a fun idea. And when I was planning my clothes with Em and Jed, the pink babydoll dress, pigtails and sequinned platform sneakers had seemed funny.

Now, seeing myself through Viggo's eyes, I felt silly and a bit trashy.

I was expecting him to look shocked, disgusted even. But instead, he smiled and opened his black jacket to reveal a lurid blue swirly top, gold neck-chains and, as I looked down, I saw he wore lime green polyester pants and chunky platform sneakers.

"I have no idea who I'm meant to be," he said, grinning. "But my sister said these were appropriate clothes. And you look ... well, odd, but beautiful."

"Really?" I breathed.

"Really. I'm so glad you invited me, Constance. Because ... and I know

I haven't even entered the party yet, so this may seem forward, but I could either ask now or spend all evening anticipating the perfect moment and —you know me—I do prefer to just come out and say these things so: oddly-dressed Constance Chase, I would like very much to ask you to be my girlfriend."

TWENTY-EIGHT

"That's how he asked you?"

Jed and I are sitting on the kiosk counter, peering out at the semi-dark skate rink. It looks kind of pretty like this, all dim and shadowy, the light from the Coke fridges illuminating the metal rails so they glitter and shine.

My skates are on the counter on either side of me and I have a hand in each. I'm running them idly backwards and forwards on the Laminex surface. I'm in a sombre mood now, thinking of that night when Viggo and I became "Congo" and how, exactly a year later, I royally screwed it up.

"Yeah," I say quietly. "That's how he asked me."

"What an absolute prick," Jed spits.

I turn to him, mouth open. "What? What's that supposed to mean? It was romantic!"

"It was a business transaction!" Jed cries. "He asked you to be his girlfriend as if he was employing you to be his secretary."

"That's not true! It was lovely! And he made a huge effort, dressing like a boy band member. And he bought me a present."

"What present?" Jed asks. "Oh no, wait. This I remember. He

bought you a CD, didn't he? One hundred greatest classical songs of all time? Something like that?"

I feel my cheeks colour. "Yes," I say defensively. "And he bought me a book on John Howard. What's wrong with that?"

"He asks you to be his girlfriend and then gives you a book on John Howard."

I look down at my toes. I haven't put my Vans back on. My feet are in mismatched socks—one spotted, the other one with tiny chickens on it.

Viggo would have a cow. He hates things that don't match.

"Can I tell you the next memory already?" I ask. "This one is more romantic."

Jed gives me a funny look. "We need to leave," he says. "It's six am. Meg is opening at six-thirty, with another guy. We obviously can't be here when they arrive."

"Okay," I say. "So what's the next adventure? Where are you taking me now?"

"Do you really want to keep doing this?" Jed snaps. "I mean, it's not even Christmas anymore. I'm tired. I'm sure you're tired. Maybe we should both just go home."

I stare at Jed for a moment. "What's wrong?" I ask finally. I hold up a finger when he opens his mouth. "Don't tell me nothing's wrong, Jeremiah. I know something's wrong. I know you better than I know anybody in the world. I know when you're not okay."

"You know me better than you know Viggo?"

I suck in a breath and think how to phrase my answer. "I mean, I've known you *longer*, so—"

"And, point of fact—" Jed hops off the counter and strides over to where he left his boots. He shoves his feet in and begins doing up the metal clips. "You don't know when I'm not okay. You used to, but for the past year you've had no idea."

"What does that mean?"

"Do you want to just go home?" He glances up at me. He does look tired. "I'm actually kind of over this."

"Jed, please just tell me what's wrong," I plead, moving towards him. I hold out my hand to take his. He ignores it. "Come on, Jeremiah. This isn't like you. Why are you acting all funny?"

"Why am—" Jed shakes his head. "Connie, you're the one who acted like you were kidnapped by the Shakri and replaced with an überclone for a *whole entire year*, and you ask me why *I'm* acting funny?"

He puffs out an angry breath. "Connie, I came over to your house last night so we could have a good old bitch together about Viggo and how he done you wrong and when you said you had all these memories of him, I thought, 'yeah, let's share some bad memories of Viggo. Have a really good, solid, ranty, angry—probably quite humorous and entertaining—debrief. But instead, you're still all starry-eyed, even though Blind Freddie could see Viggo was a total dick to you. Even before you were together. Which is as far as we've got so far. We've only just got to him 'formally proposing that you become his girlfriend', and already I'm torn between hating the guy and being bored witless."

"He's meant to be your best friend," I protest feebly.

"*Was* meant to be my best friend," Jed corrects. "We were friends when we were kids. And then we kept in touch and saw each other once in a blue moon and that was kind of fine because I didn't stay long enough for him to ditch me. Or for him to annoy the Ewok out of me, which is all he's been doing since he came back. Now I want to punch his lights out."

"And you've felt this way for … a year? Why … why did you keep being friends with him then?"

Jed fixes me with a piercing, withering stare. "Because you loved him, dumb arse. And I didn't want to lose you."

He walks past me towards the exit.

"Jed?" I call after him. "Where are you going?"

He turns. He really does look exhausted. "*We* are going, Connie-girl. We are going to go and get a really greasy, disgusting McDonald's breakfast and I'm going to stop being such an emo and you're going to tell me more about the delightful Viggo MacDuff."

I take his arm and we leave together. "I'll prove to you he's not so bad," I say.

"I'll let you try," Jed says.

TWENTY-NINE

Memory 17

The day after my birthday party, Viggo turned up on my doorstep.

I didn't answer the door because I was still in bed. The party had ended at midnight and Mum and Dad and I had kept the bad nineties' music going and cleaned up the house. I didn't get to bed until nearly two. And, don't get me wrong; this wasn't, like, "the latest I'd ever stayed up" or anything pathetic like that. Jed and I had stayed awake till sunrise heaps of times, binge-watching box sets or listening to music or just talking into the wee hours. I was used to late nights and zombie mornings, but, nonetheless, after a two am bedtime, it's nice to just stay in bed until you feel human, or until someone brings you doughnuts.

Nobody brought me doughnuts. So in bed I stayed.

Ergo, it was Mum who answered the door to Viggo at nine am.

Yep, you heard that right. At nine on a Sunday morning, Viggo was already showered, dressed and had bicycled the at-least-half-hour trip to my house.

The man is not human.

Of course, it helped that he left the party at nine pm, citing an application deadline for university summer school.

"Poppet, you have a visitor!"

I dragged myself, grumbling, down the stairs, bleary eyed and bed-haired and still dressed in my Dalek pyjamas.

"If this is you, Jeremiah, you better have doughnuts," I muttered.

It was, of course, not Jed. Because it was nine am on a freaking Sunday morning.

It was, instead and of course, Viggo MacDuff. All shiny and dressed in a suit and tie.

Yes, Viggo MacDuff cycles in a suit.

"Poppet?" My dad was standing at the door, his expression a combination of amused and befuddled.

He was also wearing his Sunday Best: stubbie shorts, Ugg boot slippers, a faded "Come on, Aussie, Come on!" tee-shirt, circa nineteen eighty-five, and a Boags Beer hat.

There was a ridiculous amount of not good happening all at once.

I threw my dad a murderous look, which I hoped said, "Do not embarrass me any more than I already am. And do not call me Poppet again!"

Dad grinned again, his eyes flashing wickedly. "Poppet, this bloke says he's your new boyfriend. You been keeping something from your old dad?"

"Only since last night," I mumbled. I took a deep breath. "Dad, Viggo. Viggo, my dad, Steve."

"We have already done introductions while you continued your beauty sleep," Viggo said, smiling indulgently. "Fetching outfit, new girlfriend."

"I swear I don't usually … I just … it was late and …" I blathered.

"She's telling the truth." I turned around to see my little sister standing behind me, also still in her pyjamas. "Constance usually dresses for bed in a trés elegant Egyptian cotton Laura Ashley nightgown."

Patience's face was deadpan. She wasn't trying to make fun of me. She was trying to help.

Did I mention I adore my little sister?

"I'm certain Constance did not intend to look so unappealing," Viggo said. "Not all of us are out our best at …" He looked at his watch. "Well, I can't really say it's first thing in the morning anymore."

"*Constance doesn't look unappealing!*" Patience protested. "*She looks phenomenal. She always does!*"

"*I'll just go and get changed into something more … less … like this,*" I said, trying to smile. I'm sure it looked more like a grimace.

"*No matter,*" Viggo said, holding up a hand. "*I only came over to drop off the university summer school prospectus. I decided, as I worked on my own application, that it was essential that you accompany me.*"

"*You're doing summer school?*" my dad asked, raising a curious eyebrow. "*I thought you and Jed were going up the coast with his family. Didn't I hear you and your mum talking about Wineglass Bay?*"

"*I'm certain those plans can change,*" Viggo said, his teeth gleaming. "*Constance, I believe it is imperative to the betterment of your education during this coming—final—year of matriculation to undertake some additional tertiary classes at university level. I also believe that associating with those already engaged in these opportunities for educational extension would see you in good stead for your university studies in the coming years, and provide you with a more rounded conception of the courses on offer to you upon enrolment.*"

I blinked.

My dad blinked.

I cleared my throat. "Um. Yeah. What he said."

Patience grinned. "Good one, Connie! I can help you with the work, if you like. I've already been doing a few uni subjects in my spare time. It'll be fun."

Did I mention my sister is a child prodigy?

Dad looked at me quizzically. "Well, then, 'Constance'," he said slowly, his lip twitching. *"Far be it from me to stand in the way of your educational betterment. If you don't mind, I think I'll go and … better myself. Out in the garden. With The Age and a strong coffee. Great to meet you, mate,"* he said, holding out a hand to Viggo, who shook firmly.

"*And you, sir. I look forward to many of these exchanges in the future.*"

As my father walked away, I was sure I could see his shoulders shaking with silent giggles. I shook my head.

Accountants. They have seriously screwy senses of humour. There was nothing vaguely funny about Viggo MacDuff. He was perfection.

"Well, I'll leave you two to it," said Patience, backing away. "I've got extra advanced biology to do. Hurrah!"

Patience wasn't being sarcastic. Additional homework is my sister's idea of heaven. She literally skipped away.

Viggo beamed at me. "Your young sister seems like an exceptional person."

"She is," I said proudly. "So …" I leaned into him, trying to forget how "unappealing" I looked. "Did you have a good night last night?

Viggo nodded emphatically. "I certainly did! I went home and spent a solid hour and a quarter boning up on my own pre-summer-school preparation …"

That wasn't exactly what I meant but … okay.

"… and then I spent a further quarter of an hour before my bedtime perusing the prospectus and marking courses I thought you might enjoy engaging in. You'll note …" His voice was suddenly softer and more tender. "I have—sneakily—marked a couple of classes I am also taking. I thought it might be a positive action if we took them together. Perhaps you could even enhance your learning by taking notes for both of us, and we could consolidate your information acquirement by way of—perhaps—you reiterating the main points of the lecturer to me in a post-lecture study session?"

I didn't hear anything but "together" and "post-lecture study session".

My heart swelled.

For a moment, I forgot about bed-hair.

I forgot about my daggy PJs.

I forgot about Wineglass Bay, and how I actually had been looking forward to going there with Jed, and how he was probably going to be a bit peeved that I wasn't going.

I forgot all of that and concentrated instead on moving towards my boyfriend—Viggo MacDuff—and pulling him close.

"Thank you," I said. "For taking the time to do that for me."

His voice was a whisper in my ear. "No problem whatsoever, Constance.

It was my pleasure. I enjoy helping you to find the best self you could possibly be. Even more so now we are ..."

I pulled back slowly and looked him in the eye (which involved craning my neck quite a bit—Viggo was gorgeously tall). "We ... are ...?"

"We are," Viggo said firmly.

And then he pulled me back to him.

And pressed his lips to mine.

And we kissed.

I.

Kissed.

Viggo.

MacDuff.

Oh Ben Folds.

THIRTY

"Yep. Okay. TMI right there."

Jed and I are sitting in McDonalds. He's halfway through a mouthful of Big Mac.

I have a strong coffee … and an Oreo McFlurry.

There's no way Jed would let me order an ordinary breakfast. I'm glad. Jed Food seems to be helping soothe my savaged soul and, since living on alfalfa and lean chicken breast for the year I was with Viggo, my body is giving me a high five for all the bad fats and carbohydrates. Sadly, however, one McFlurry can't take the pain away entirely. Thinking about my first kiss with Viggo has made my chest go all funny. There are pinpricks at the back of my eyes.

I don't reply to Jed, just shovel another heaped spoonful in my mouth and shrug.

"Sorry," he says after a moment. "I guess that was a difficult memory to relive."

"Yup," I reply after swallowing.

"I won't be too hard on you about cancelling the East Coast trip I was really looking forward to then."

"Please don't be."

"If you don't mind me asking, though ... was the kiss ... I mean ... Did you ..."

"Did I like it?" I ask, reading Jed's mind. "Of course I—"

But then I stop. And I try to remember. To *really* remember.

And I find I can't. I can remember Viggo leaning in. I can remember him pressing his lips to mine. I can remember he smelled of his fancy Ralph Lauren aftershave. I can remember feeling excited, flattered ...

But the actual kiss itself?

"Of course I did," I say, ignoring the strange, uncertain feeling in my belly. "It was Viggo. Of course he was a good kisser."

I know this part at least is true. Because obviously that first kiss wasn't the *only* kiss I shared with Viggo MacDuff. He kissed me lots of times after. After he gave speeches or accepted awards he'd always come back to me and kiss me on the cheek. I liked those kisses—the public ones—because it showed the world I was Viggo MacDuff's girlfriend. I belonged to him. Of course he kissed me in private, too. He kissed me goodbye and goodnight whenever we parted and his kisses were just like him: firm, assured, confident. So of course that first kiss *would* have been good. I don't know why I blanked it out.

I'm just tired.

"Maybe we *should* go home," I say to Jed. "I'm starting to feel ..."

I look around the restaurant. It's full of smiling, happy people. People who had a great family Christmas yesterday, then a long, full-bellied sleep and are now having a special Boxing Day treat. The restaurant is still decked out in Christmas tinsel and there's a plastic tree in the corner. Everything and everyone feels festive. Nobody here has just had their heart broken.

I'm the only one.

I'm all alone.

And I'm suddenly very, very tired.

"No."

I look at Jed curiously. "No? What do you mean no?"

"No, you're not going to bed." There is a glint in Jed's eye.

"But you're the one who was suggesting it, back at the roller skating rink," I point out.

"Yeah, I was being a dumbarse," Jed says. He takes a final bite of his Big Mac and wipes the grease on his jeans. "You're not going to bed, Connie-girl. We will go to your house, but only so you can get a jumper and some less-precious shoes."

"That sounds ominous. Is this for another adventure?" The strange, sick feeling in my belly is transforming into a buzzing excitement. Why would I need a jumper in the middle of summer? Where is Jed going to take me?

"It sure is," says Jed. "Well, not so much of an adventure. More of a reliving of another memory. A memory that's not of Viggo MacDuff or 'Congo'. I think we need a break from memories of Viggo MacDuff, just for an hour or two. I think we need to remember one of our great moments. A memory of Jed and Connie."

"'Jennie'?" I grin.

"'Coned'," he corrects, pronouncing it like "conehead". I like it.

"Sounds good to me. Let's go." I stand up from the table and offer Jed my hand.

As we walk out of the restaurant, my phone buzzes again in my pocket. I ignore it. All of that can wait. The rest of the world can wait.

Even Viggo MacDuff can wait.

Suddenly, all I want is this: me and Jed and memories of before Viggo, when I was happy.

The thought stops me in my tracks.

Before Viggo.

When I was happy.

I don't really mean that … do I?

I mean before we split up.

I mean before he broke my heart.

I don't really mean I was happy before Viggo came into my life. I can't mean that.

I love Viggo MacDuff.

I love him. That's what all these memories are reinforcing for me. How great Viggo is. How clever he is. How successful he is. It's just stupid Jed putting crazy doubting feelings in my head because he has some ridiculous bee in his bonnet about Viggo. He's acting weird and it's rubbing off on me.

"Let's go," I say, attempting to shake the weird. "Let's go to my house and then let's go and do some 'Coned' remembering."

"About time," Jed mutters under his breath.

THIRTY-ONE

When we arrive home, Patience is sitting on our front doorstep. When she sees us walking towards the gate, she jumps up and runs towards us. "Connie Alwyn Chase, where have you been?" she asks, sounding much more like my grandmother than a newly teenaged girl. "I've been so worried!"

"Patty!" I wrap my little sister up in my arms. She smells like vanilla body spray and fruit toast and a bit like Beezus, who I realise is curled up sleeping on the step. "What are you doing home, darling? I thought you guys were staying at Auntie Barbara's until tomorrow."

Patience sticks her bottom lip out. "I missed you. Mum and Dad got sick of me complaining, so we came home."

"Oh, Pitter-Patter." I kiss her on the cheek. "They didn't mind coming home early?"

Patience shakes her head. "Auntie Barbara hates cricket so it's banned in her house, even on Boxing Day. I think Dad was desperate for an excuse to leave. He would have been distraught if he'd missed the test! So anyway, what are we going to do today?"

"Um—" I look at Jed. He smiles and shrugs.

"We're doing this thing," he says. "See, Connie broke up with Viggo and—"

Patience's face breaks into a huge grin. "Seriously? You and the douchebucket broke up? Oh frabjous day! Callooh Callay!"

My mouth is wide open.

I've have never, not once, not ever, heard my little sister swear. For a moment, this is the only part of what she just said that sinks in. Then it hits me; it wasn't just random swearing. It was swearing about Viggo. "Wait—what did you just say?" I gasp.

I realise that, next to me, Jed is doubled over, his shoulders heaving with silent giggles. I elbow him in the shoulder and he straightens, biting his lip. His face is the colour of the poppies in Mum's garden.

"I said Viggo MacDuff is a douchebucket," Patience says, sticking her chin out. "And I'm glad you broke up with him. About time. So are we going to celebrate then? Shall we go and have cake?"

I am too gobsmacked to say a word in reply. Even though there is the possibility of cake.

"Connie? Cake?" Jed prompts. When I still don't answer, Jed says, "I'm sure cake will factor somewhere in our adventures, Patty C. You're welcome to join us."

"Marvellous!" says Patience, grinning. "Where are we going?"

"Ah. Now, see, that would ruin the surprise for your sister," Jed says. "But I will tell you that you should go and find a pair of hiking boots, and a thick jumper, and find some for Connie as well."

"Easy!" Patience says, skipping up the steps. "Sounds intriguing! I can't wait. As long as I don't have to hear one word about Viggo MacDuff while we do ... whatever it is we're doing ... I'll be happy. Unless it's a swear word! Oh Connie. I have never been so jubilant! This is the best Boxing Day ever!"

"Ah, now see ..." Jed calls after Patience. "There's the catch.

You *do* have to hear about Viggo. We're reliving every moment of 'Congo's' relationship in minute detail. Twenty-five whole memories, all about him."

Patience stops, twirls and grimaces. Then she looks thoughtful. Then she smirks. "Okay," she says slowly. "That's okay. I'm sure if we're reliving memories of Viggo MacDuff, I'll find plenty there to bitch about. This could be great fun! I'll see you in a minute."

My eyes are bulging again. First she's calling Viggo a totally inexplicable swear word. Now she's looking forward to *bitching* about him? What has happened to my angelic little sister?

And what on Earth did Viggo do to make her act like that?

Jed grins. "Guess I'm not the only one who's a bit anti-Viggo today."

"A bit?" I finally gasp. "Jed ... if *Patience* doesn't like Viggo, maybe ... maybe there's actually something ..."

"I guess we'll find out as we relive some more memories whether Viggo MacDuff actually is a 'douchebucket'." Jed suppresses a laugh. "But remember we're having a bit of Viggo-free time while we have this next adventure."

"That's ... fine."

I feel shaken.

I just assumed Patience loved Viggo. I assumed my whole family loved Viggo. I *assumed* they were proud of me, for landing myself such an ambitious and successful boyfriend, for getting my act together and buckling down at school and dressing nicely and all the other things that had come as a side-effect of my relationship with Viggo.

I assumed he had charmed them like he charmed me.

I mean, why wouldn't everyone love Viggo MacDuff?

Even after what happened at the party, I never for a moment stopped loving Viggo MacDuff and that was the first time he had ever been less than ... perfect.

What happened at the party was the only thing that could ever make anyone think that Viggo MacDuff wasn't completely fabulous. Or at least I'd thought that. But Jed keeps making all these cutting little remarks and now my Pollyanna of a sister is calling him a …

I can't even say that word again.

I feel sick. Patience never thought badly of anyone and she thought badly of Viggo MacDuff.

I swallow. My hand goes to my fluttery belly. "Jed," I say weakly. "Why does Patty think Viggo is a … Why do you? I thought Viggo MacDuff was perfect."

"He is. Like I said. And that's exactly the problem."

"I didn't understand that the last time you said it," I say. "Isn't being perfect a good thing?"

"Are we ready to go?"

Patience is walking out the front door, her arms full of woolly jumpers and hiking shoes. "Let's get this show on the road," she says. "Yay! I'm so excited!"

I take a brown jumper from her arms and Jed takes one of Dad's. As I pull mine on, I hear Patience say something to Jed. I can't make out exactly what it is, but when my head pops out the neck-hole, I hear Jed's response.

He's looking at me intently. "Yes, I saw them," he says. "I hope so too."

I look down to see that my tee-shirt has come untucked. My ribs are bare.

I pull my shirt and jumper down quickly but it's too late.

He saw them.

So did she.

But they don't know. They can't know. Even if they suspect …

They won't suspect. And if they do …

I'll tell them the truth.

That I deserved it.

"Can we go now?" I ask briskly. "I've got a heap more memories to get through. And I want to see where Jed is taking us that needs jumpers in the middle of summer."

Jed and Patience exchange a look.

I ignore them. "Come on already," I say. "I'm long overdue for an adventure."

THIRTY-TWO

W e're up the top of a mountain.

Of course we are. Where else would we need boots and woolly knits in December?

Jed got Tallulah working and he drove us to the lookout, and then we climbed.

And it is cold up here. So cold it feels like snow. So cold my skin is tingling through layers of fleece and heavy denim. So cold I can see my breath puffing white in the air in front of me. So cold Patience is gripping my arms and leaning into me to try to keep warm.

Viggo would call it "frigid" or "biting" or, if he was in a particularly good mood, "brisk" or "bracing".

I think of all those words as I hike along the track with my sister and my best friend. But the words that came out of my mouth are, "Ben Folds, it's bloody freezing."

"Now now, Connie-girl. Use your polite words," Jed says, and I'm relieved to see he's smiling. He's been looking tense ever since I put my jumper on, ever since my top rode up, ever since …

But he's forgotten. Hopefully. Or he's decided it—they—aren't worth worrying about.

Or, like me, he's just so transfixed by our surroundings—so utterly dumbfounded that there's a place like this so close to our suburban home—that nothing else seems to matter anymore.

Of course, we've been up here before, on a school trip when Jed and I were little, but all I remember is that there *was* snow that day, and Jed and I made a snowman called Percy, and we saw a wombat bottom poking out of its hole.

I don't remember being awestruck by the sheer awesomeness of this place. I guess you don't really notice that sort of thing when you're eleven years old. But now, at seventeen, I'm so moved by the beauty around me that I'm almost crying.

I'm almost crying, and it has nothing to do with Viggo MacDuff.

In fact, for the first time since we broke up …

For the first time since we *met* …

Nothing is about Viggo MacDuff.

I haven't thought about him in at least half an hour, and this realisation shocks me. I thought he was so much a part of me, so embedded in my brain, that I'd never be able to stop thinking about him, even for a minute, let alone a whole thirty of them.

"You look … pensive," says Patience. She notices my raised eyebrow. "What? It's one of my words of the week for English. It means thoughtful. But you probably already know that. Viggo probably taught you, right? The Human Thesaurus."

"No, Connie was *always* an English nerd," Jed corrects Patience. "Viggo is the Human Textbook."

"Actually, *is* he even human?" Patience asks, all innocence. "I have been suspecting for some time that he is, in fact, a robot."

"Why did I never know you didn't like Viggo?" I ask, nudging Patience in the ribs. "You never told me."

"As if I was going to tell you when you were still blissfully, head-over-heels in love with him!" Patience cries. "You would have hated me. But now you've broken up ... oh, it feels so good to say it. I hate him." She raises her voice. "I hate Viggo MacDuff!"

Above us, a flock of cockatoos takes flight from a tree. Patience laughs. "See, they hate him too. Just the mention of his name and they're off."

"Why did you hate him?" I ask.

Patience shrugs. "Same reason everyone does. He's a total smarmy, arrogant, obnoxious, domineering, stick-up-his-bum, classical-music-loving, fun-hating *bastard!*"

I'm genuinely shocked. "Patience!"

Patience puts a hand to her mouth. "Oops. Not one of my words of the week for English. But very apt."

"It's okay, Pitter-patter," I murmur. "I just want you to explain to me why you think that." I glance at Jed. "And tell me why you do, too. Tell me why everyone hates Viggo MacDuff. Make me see it. Persuade me. Maybe then it will all hurt less."

Jed shakes his head. "You need to work it out yourself."

Patience nods. "Tell us some more memories," she says. "Maybe you'll find one where Viggo isn't so wonderful."

"I haven't yet," I mutter. "Jed seems to think the memories prove Viggo is bad, but I can't see it. He's just as smart and charismatic and handsome and driven and *wonderful* in my memories as when I was living them."

"Keep going," Patience says, her voice more serious now. Her eyes drift down to my ribs. "Keep telling them. Tell us everything. I'm sure, eventually, you'll work it out."

THIRTY-THREE

We sit on a log, watching currawongs bounce and bob along on the undergrowth. "They look so happy," I sigh. "So happy in their little, bouncy world. I guess currawongs don't fall in love."

"Maybe they do," Patience says. "Or maybe they know better. Maybe they know that boys suck."

"Oi!" Jed says. "Right here, Patty!"

Patience rolls her eyes. "You're not a boy, Jed."

"Thanks very much." Jed feigns hurt before grinning. He gestures at the bird. "Besides, how do you know it's a female currawong? It could be Colin the currawong for all you know."

"It's a female," I say. When Jed and Patience both look at me quizzically, I explain. "The females have shorter beaks."

"Viggo?" Patience asks dryly. I nod.

"He likes bird-watching."

"But that's an 'outdoors pursuit'," Jed says, aping Viggo again. I have to admit, he does a pretty good impersonation.

And it is kind of annoying.

"I know. Viggo doesn't do outdoors pursuits," I say. "Unless they're mandated by Young Rotary. But he won a bird-watching day as part of a science prize a few years back. And of course, even though he didn't want to do it, he fully committed to it and did it *well*. He can still reel off all the names. I don't think he actually goes actively bird-watching anymore. Not, like, in nature. But he still knows everything about them. In fact, there are birds in my next memory of him. Seagulls. No, wait, *silver* gulls—the most common sea bird in Australia. Scientific name 'Chroicocephalus novaehollandiae'."

"You actually remember that?"

I nod miserably at my sister. "I remember everything. But wait —" I look at Jed. "You said coming here on this adventure related to a Connie-and-Jed—a *Coned*—memory."

"Snowmen," he says. "The wombat. Don't you remember?"

I nod. My lips twitch. "Yes, I remember."

"We had an awesome time that day. One of the best days of my life. Just Connie and Jed, doing our thing."

I look at him curiously. "Seriously?"

"Yep. And on the bus on the way home, we worked out how we were going to get a Tardis."

"We did too." I laugh. And I do remember now, how much fun I had. How free and boundless I felt that day with Jed.

How I almost always felt that way, with Jed.

"So tell me about Viggo and seagulls," he says.

And I suddenly feel deflated. Because I didn't feel boundless in this memory. I didn't feel free that day.

"All right," I say. "So, we went to the beach. And yes, it was an outdoor pursuit, but we weren't there for fun."

THIRTY-FOUR

Memory 18

It was the start of the new school year. Viggo and I had spent the summer doing classes at the university. I'd done sessions in Australian, American and British politics and British military history. I'd wanted to do a couple of art and music classes too, but there hadn't been time once Viggo had planned my schedule. But that was okay. I learned a lot, and I got to spend time with Viggo.

When we got back to normal school, as well as all the other clubs Viggo and I were involved in, Viggo signed us up for the Landcare group.

I was surprised, at the time, by his choice. The only time I'd ever heard him talk about environmental issues was to dismiss those who cared about them.

"You're either an environmentalist or you're for progress." He waved his hand in the air. "You can't be both. I'm for progress all the way. Greenies can whinge all they want about old growth forests and special, unique species of bush grub, but economic growth must take precedence. When I am in power—" Viggo said this a lot, and I always marvelled at his complete certainty that he would, one day, be running this country. He was so confident. I was in awe. "—I will be about seeing business thrive in this country, not letting it wither and die in the name of 'saving the planet'. Global warming is a myth, anyway. Everyone knows …"

The old Connie would have argued with him, but I knew better than to try. Viggo was a hugely successful debater. There was no point attempting to win an argument with him and, besides, I didn't really want to. It was so much nicer when I just agreed with Viggo, even if, inside, I didn't really. There was no harm in pretending, if it kept the peace. Viggo tended to get a bit … heated if you disagreed with him. He was passionate about his beliefs. It was one of his many great character traits.

Which is exactly why I was so surprised when he told me he was the new Vice President of the Bangarra High Landcare Group. Until he explained. "Diversity," he said. "We can't have all our eggs in the one basket. What if someone on the university selection panel happened to be on the board of Keep Australia Beautiful?" He prodded a fingertip into his palm. "Which is why—naturally—you will be joining the group too, won't you, Constance?"

I had actually been thinking of joining Landcare the previous year —before Viggo arrived—but I was put off when I found out all of the über-clones had already joined. I knew exactly why they'd signed up. And it all had to do with Ryan Chapman.

Ryan Chapman was the president of the Bangarra High Landcare group. And Ryan Chapman was the Hottest-Boy-In-School. And there was nothing a überclone loved more than a Hottest-Boy-In-School.

Jed and I had laughed together about it all. The shallowness! The lack of actual social conscience! The incurable superficiality of the überclone!

Since I'd started shopping at the boutique where Kacey worked, and she'd found out I was friends with her cousin Em, the überclones were actually being really nice to me. And they could be surprisingly kind of fun to hang around. Kacey and I were almost … friends.

She was nice.

It could be fun, spending more time with her in the Landcare group. And spending more time with Viggo would be brilliant, of course.

There was only one problem …

"No time?" Viggo said tersely. "Too many extracurriculars already? Constance, as you know, there is always a solution. Where there is a will, there is a way! We will simply forgo our weekend brunches to help out. We can move our book-discussions to Thursday lunchtimes. Which reminds me: how are you going with the Richard Nixon biography?"

I hadn't started it.

"Great!" I said.

And then I sat up until two am and read the whole thing.

Patience helped me to apply my under-eye concealer, so Viggo wouldn't notice my dark shadows. He didn't like me to look tired.

THIRTY-FIVE

Memory 19

So with concealed under-eyes and my perkiest smile, I joined the Bangarra High Landcare Group at Bangarra Beach clutching a long metal rubbish-grabber in my hand along with everyone else.

Well, everyone else except Viggo, that is.

He was "coordinating". Ryan was away at leadership camp, so Viggo was in charge. And in charge is where Viggo prefers to be. He was positively bouncing.

He'd made Kacey his second-in-command.

I was trying to hide my disappointment. I knew Viggo must have a strategy. Some sort of political reason for promoting Kacey. And she did seem to be taking her role seriously, racing around to relay Viggo's instructions to the rest of us.

She was doing a good job.

She was also wearing a boob tube. And teeny-tiny denim shorts. And looked like a Sports Illustrated model.

Whereas I was dressed in the outfit Viggo had picked for me—three-quarter length navy capri pants, a khaki button-down shirt, sensible black lace-up boat shoes and a navy cardigan around my shoulders. I knew I looked elegant. I knew Viggo approved of my outfit.

I knew I'd look ridiculous in a boob tube, even a posh one from Kacey's boutique, and that I really didn't have the figure for cutoffs, but still …

Did she have to be walking quite so closely to Viggo in that outfit?

Not that I thought for a moment Viggo would look twice at her in that way. Viggo was "attracted to a brain, not a body".

And he liked my brain. I knew that.

I didn't know if he liked my body, too, but I assumed he did.

I mean, sure, we hadn't really progressed past kissing—which we did as often as Viggo had time—but he spent so much time helping me plan my outfits and fixing my hair …

He must be attracted to me to do all that. Mustn't he?

As if he was reading my mind and sensing my insecurities, Viggo turned and looked back at me. "Constance? Can you come and help us?"

I raced forwards, breaking up a gang of silver gulls, who were fighting over a discarded bucket of chips.

I bounced up to Viggo, offering my cheek for a kiss. Viggo shook his head. "Did you not see the takeaway food rubbish?" he hissed at me.

"Oh, sorry." I turned on my heel, raced back to the chip bucket, rubbish-grabbed it up and into my Glad bag, and sped back to Viggo's side. He was smiling again now.

"Hi, honey," I said, grinning back.

Viggo winced. "Professionalism, Constance," he said, his eyes darting to Kacey.

My chest tightened. I forced a professional smile.

Viggo cleared his throat. "Anyway, I was wondering if you might run us an errand?"

"Sure!" My chest loosened. Viggo did value my contribution after all! I knew he was only making Kacey his second-in-command for strategic reasons. He was going to give me an important job—one that Kacey couldn't manage.

I knew he had faith in me.

"Kacey has a pain in her ankle," Viggo went on. "I need you to go to the nearest chemist shop and procure her some painkillers. Paracetemol, not Ibuprofen, as this gives her a stomach ache. Take the cost out of your own funds and Landcare will reimburse you."

"Oh. Okay."

"Sorry," Kacey mouthed. I gave her a half-smile and then turned to walk away, feeling deflated.

But then …

"Constance?"

I looked over my shoulder. Viggo's arms were open and his sea-green eyes were twinkling at me. I felt a rush of warmth. I sprinted towards him, towards his open arms. He clamped me firmly by the shoulders. "Thank you," he said gently. "I know it's not a glamorous job, any of this, but I appreciate you doing it. You're a great girl, Constance Chase."

"You're a great girl, Constance Chase," Jed and Patience parrot.

"What?" I ask, unable to wipe the grin from my face despite their mocking. "Viggo thought I was a great girl." My shoulders slump. "Thought. Past tense. He doesn't think it anymore."

"Then he's a bast—"

"Patience!" I snap. "Can you a) stop using nasty words—you are far too young and clever to be talking like that, and b) stop applying them to Viggo. He is not a bast … bad person. Has everyone forgotten this whole breakup is my fault? I'm the one in the wrong here, not Viggo! You should both be saying that I'm a … bad person instead. Besides, were either of you even listening to that memory? In it, Viggo not only joined an environmental cause, he displayed great leadership capabilities, he knew the scientific name for sea birds, he helped me with my fashion decisions, he was helpful to an injured person, and he called me 'great'. That memory does nothing but show how wonderful Viggo MacDuff was. *Is.* Viggo MacDuff *is* wonderful. He is, at this very moment, out there *being* wonderful. Without … me."

Tears are rolling freely down my cheeks. I don't even bother to try to stop them. I can cry in front of Patience and Jed. They are the only people in this world—apart from my parents and Beezus—who I do feel comfortable crying in front of.

I never would have cried in front of Viggo. Viggo hates weakness. Viggo hates tears.

Except, of course, I did cry, didn't I? That last night. The night of my party.

The night I wrecked the world.

"Do you want to get off this mountain?" Jed asks gently. "Maybe there's too much quiet up here. Too much space for reflection. Maybe what we need is some noise."

THIRTY-SIX

Jed shakes the hand of the guy in the tight red tee-shirt and baggy pants. The tee-shirt says, "I've never had to knock on wood, but I know someone who has".

I get the reference: it's a song by The Mighty Mighty Bosstones. I'm not sure many people our age would have even heard of that band. But this guy has not only heard of them, he likes them enough to have a tee-shirt. Which is part of the reason I am immediately intrigued.

The other part is that Jed has brought us to some sort of old, disused warehouse, between a muffler repair service and a pie factory. The whole place smells of pastry and petrol.

There's a sign on the door that says, "Keep out unless you are Doctor Worm (and if you are … Good morning! How are you?)." Again, I know what that means. It's a song by They Might Be Giants.

The guy in the red tee-shirt catches me checking out the sign. "You like TMBG?" he asks, abbreviating the band's name to show that he is a true fan.

I nod. "Yeah. Especially their early stuff."

The guy nods at Jed, obviously impressed. I feel proud. "Dude," he says. "I think we got a live one here."

I know I'm grinning like an idiot. Why does it feel so cool that this guy I don't even know is impressed by the fact I like a semi-obscure indie band?

The guy turns to Patience. "Hey, kiddo, do you share your big sister's awesome taste in music?"

She shakes her head. "Nope, sorry. I'm just your typical thirteen-year-old. Total Swifty." She smiles. "Sorry to disappoint."

He shakes his head. "Not at all. I totally rate Taylor Swift. Awesome songwriter. We won't be playing any in our set, though. Sorry to disappoint *you.*"

Our set?

I look quizzically at Jed. The guy catches it. "Ah! I forgot Jed said in his text you'll have no idea why you're here," he says, smirking. "Welcome to the home of Barenaked Ween. We're a nineties' cover band. For now. Until we hit the big time and they let us play our own songs. Your mate here has been filling in on some drums for us the past few months. He's great on Korn and System Of A Down. And you should hear him rock Alien Ant Farm's 'Smooth Criminal'. He's got some wicked lyric ideas too, for when we make the crossover. We're thinking we might just keep him on."

Jed's mouth drops open. "Really? *Dude ...*"

I know my mouth's open too. Jed? In a nineties' cover band?

"How did I not know this?" I ask.

"You've been ... preoccupied," he mutters.

"But Jed? Really? You hate nineties' music."

The guy laughs. "Like hell he does. This guy has an encyclopaedic knowledge. He's a nineties' music Rain Man."

Jed shrugs. "You kinda got me into it. Don't tell my metal friends though, okay?"

I shake my head. "I really have missed out on your life, haven't I? While I've been with Viggo."

Jed shrugs again. He turns back to the guy. "Connie, this is Gus. Gus, Constance Chase."

"Awesome name," says Gus, holding out his hand. "Sounds like an album title. You prefer Connie, though?"

I'm caught off-guard by the question, and I have to take a moment to think about it. I always did prefer Connie, before Viggo, but he convinced me Constance sounded more grown-up and professional.

I never did really feel like it fit me, though, did I? It was like the suits and the heels—stiff, restrictive, uncomfortable. Not *me*.

"I prefer Connie." I ignore the nagging feeling of *disobedience* that swells inside me as I say it.

It feels as if I am betraying Viggo.

In fact, I feel as if I'm betraying Viggo by even being here, in this place he would have called "dingy".

I feel as if I am betraying him by talking to Gus—Viggo didn't really like me talking to other males unless it was for "professional or educational reasons".

I feel as if I betrayed him by colouring my hair blue, by putting on my Snoopy Vans the day after we broke up …

I look at my feet.

Why *did* I put on my Vans the day after we broke up?

What was I thinking? What the hell is wrong with me? No wonder Viggo doesn't want to be with me anymore. I'm hopeless. I'm weak. I'm …

"You ready to rock?" Gus asks. As he smiles, light glints off his lower lip and I see he has a silver stud pierced through it. His septum is pierced too.

I stop myself thinking it looks cool. It doesn't look cool. How will he ever get a proper job with something like that in his face?

That's what Viggo would say, if he was here.

I wish Viggo was here. I wish it so hard.

He'd put a stop to all this nonsense. He'd pull me into line again, get me back into shape. He'd—

I look over and notice Jed is already seated at the drums. I feel a hand on my elbow.

"You okay, Connie?" Gus asks softly. "You don't look like you want to be here. But … if you don't mind me saying this, from everything Jed has told me about you—and the guy never, ever shuts up about you—I think you *belong* here."

Jed is fiddling with a screw on the hi-top cymbals. He doesn't see me looking. But Gus does.

"*Never* stops talking about you," he repeats. When I catch his eye again, he winks. "So, do you want to be here, Connie? Because we're about to rock this popsicle stand and it won't be the same without you." He points to the mic stand at the front of the group of guys—two on guitar, one on keys.

I look at him, aghast. He's not seriously saying that *I* …

"Jed says you have a good voice," says Gus, shrugging. "And I've been thinking for a while that we could do with a female lead singer. Sub in for me so I can go get a beer after those Aerosmith songs that trash my throat; sing a few Killing Heidi and Magic Dirt tunes. Maybe some Hole … Whatcha reckon? Subject to your success in this audition, of course." He gestures at the guy with the acoustic guitar and the Oasis hoodie. "Seb?"

Seb nods. He starts plucking on the strings. I recognise the song immediately.

"You know it?"

I nod. "Yeah," I say quietly.

"Then do it."

I take a deep breath.

And I walk up to the microphone.

THIRTY-SEVEN

"You were *awesome*," Patience says for what feels like the fiftieth time.

"Thanks, Pitter-Patter." I'm still blushing. Still buzzing. Still high as a kite.

I knew every word to the song and I sang them with a voice full of all the pain and heartbreak I'd felt over the past few days.

"You were meant for me, and I was meant for you …"

Jewel isn't usually my cup of tea, musically, but I don't know a teenage girl on the planet who doesn't know the words to that song. Even if they weren't born when it was released. It's the quintessential song of breaking up.

Of lost love.

Of broken hearts and shattered dreams.

"I try and tell myself it'll be all right …"

Will it be all right?

I look around the cafe table, at my sister, at the guys from the band.

At Jed.

Barenaked Ween have asked me to join, as an occasional lead singer, to duet with Gus and sing lead in "girl" songs.

I've agreed. But only if they change their name.

"Barenaked Ween is never going to sing their own songs," I point out. "Barenaked Ween pigeonholes you as a covers band. And it kind of sounds a bit icky."

"What should we call ourselves then?" Gus asks, taking a sip of his cappuccino (*so* nineties). I raise my flat white to my lips and blow. "Hmm. I don't know. I'll think about it."

"You sure you want to do this, Connie-girl?" Jed's eyes are sparkling. He looks so excited. "I mean, don't get me wrong, I'm thrilled you're saying you want to do it but … I don't want you to agree to it just for me. You've spent a year doing stuff someone else wants you to do. It's time you just did what Connie wants to do."

I think of the next memory I was going to tell.

THIRTY-EIGHT

Memory 20

Viggo *convinced me to go to the Rotary Youth Leadership camp with him on the same weekend that the Violent Femmes were playing in Hobart.*

It wasn't too bad. In fact, some of it was kind of fun. I liked learning to play golf (even if Viggo was grumpy when I beat him). We had fun cooking dinner together, and going hiking (even if Viggo grumbled the whole way about not knowing what hiking had to do with leadership—he still hated outdoors pursuits). And the part that I'd been looking forward to telling Jed and Patience—when I'd won the Best Newcomer Award at the ceremony on the last day, and Viggo had been so proud of me—that was nice.

But I still wished the whole time that I was at the concert.

There had been no chance of me going, though. Not when Viggo wanted me to do something else.

When I'd first told this memory, to Beezus, through a mouthful of chocolate, I'd concentrated on the fun we'd had together at the camp. I'd focused on how Viggo had complimented me on my quick learning and my willingness to "dig in and get my hands dirty" in the brainstorming sessions and debates. How I'd "taken instruction" (mostly from Viggo) well.

At the time, I'd been chuffed that I'd impressed Viggo so much.

Now?

All I can think of is how much that Violent Femmes concert would have rocked.

Now, all I can think of is how much I enjoyed myself, at the microphone, singing my heart out. I will join the band. Not for Jed. For me.

"So what do you think we should change our name to?" Gus asks.

I think for a moment, and then smile.

"Memories Of A Different Me," I reply.

"Cool," Gus says. "We can call ourselves MOADM for short. Everyone will want to know what it stands for. It'll generate hype and interest. Of course, you'll generate just as much."

"Me?"

"With that funky blue hair and great clothes and that killer voice? You'll be MOADM's biggest drawcard." Gus grins. "You'll be our Gwen Stefani! Thanks for joining the MOADM team, Connie Chase. And thanks for introducing us, Jedward. I think this is going to be the beginning of something *big*."

THIRTY-NINE

Dad's there when we get home, parked in front of the telly with a Boags stubbie in one hand, the other plunged into a bag of his favourite Kettle chips. The hand is not moving. He's too transfixed. "Come on, mate!" He mutters. "Come on … come on … come on … *Yes!*"

Mum appears at my side. "He's going to give himself a heart attack," she says quietly.

"I swear I don't know why he watches it when it stresses him out so much."

Mum's eyes drift up to my hair. I self-consciously raise a hand to it. "I know," I say. "Jed made me. I'll dye it back."

"No!" Mum says quickly. "Don't do that, Connie. Please. I like it!"

I'm confused. "You always said you wished I'd just leave my hair the way it was."

Mum sighs. "When you were younger, maybe. When you were still my baby and I didn't want my baby wrecking her beautiful, natural hair colour. I got used to it. It became part of you. You haven't looked like Connie for a long time. I'm glad you're back.

But wait." She puts a hand to her chest, feigning dismay. "What *will* Viggo the Great think?"

I look at her curiously. Whenever Mum called Viggo that before, I was proud. Now I finally sense a touch of sarcasm.

Maybe Patience is right. Maybe Mum and Dad really *don't* like Viggo as much as I thought they do.

"They broke up."

Patience snakes her arms around my waist and leans her cheek on my shoulder. "Apparently Connie did something bad and Viggo dumped her and Connie is heartbroken and now, to help mend her broken heart, she is telling Jed twenty-five memories of Viggo MacDuff, which she's already told Beezus while eating advent calendar chocolate. I told you there was no point buying her an advent calendar as she'd just save it all up and eat it at the end. She does it every year. Well, apart from last year when she didn't eat the chocolate at all because Viggo doesn't approve of "the cheap stuff". Anyway, she's doing that and, while she's doing that, Jed is taking them on little adventures. Because he is awesome. He's making her do crazy things like the old Connie would have done. Don't worry, Mum, not illegal stuff ... I don't *think*. It's to make her see that she's better off without Viggo. She's a better person and has more fun. But Connie hasn't realised that yet because she's so caught up in the memories and she doesn't realise that the memories make Viggo look like a total dou— bad person. Anyway, it was Jed who convinced her to dye her hair back to awesome. *And* he talked her into joining a band!"

Patience finally takes a breath and Mum looks at me with raised eyebrows.

"Well," she says finally, and then looks behind me to where Jed is hovering in the doorway. "Jed, welcome back. It's been a long time. And thank you for looking after Connie. I assume you've been here all night?"

Jed clears his throat. "I'm sorry. I know I should have made sure Connie got some sleep …"

Mum waves a hand in the air. "Pish to sleep on Christmas. I stayed up all night drinking mulled wine and watching old home movies with my sister. I had some pretty … interesting hair of my own, back in the day. I'm just glad you were here, to look after Connie. As soon as we drove away I regretted leaving. I knew we shouldn't have left her alone. I knew something was wrong. I'm just so glad you came when we …" She clears her throat.

I narrow my eyes suspiciously. *"When we" what?*

But she goes on. "You're such a good friend to my girl. I've missed you." Mum throws her arms up. "Well, don't just stand there. Come in! Unless you have to run away to other adventures. But … if you don't mind me saying, you look like you could use a nap. Why don't the three of you go up to Connie's room and have a lie down. There will be time for more gadding about later in the day. Maybe your father and I can even join you. I could do with an adventure, and he'll need a distraction if Australia loses as badly as it looks like they're going to."

I look to Jed. My sister has already invited herself on our adventures. How will Jed feel if my parents hijack his plans as well?

"It'd be great," he says. "I'd love to have you guys come. I've missed you too. You're my spare parents. You know, for when the real parentals are finally revealed to be Stepford robots. It's been lonely without y'all. But, in the interests of transparency, my next challenge does involve getting tattoos."

Mum blanches.

"Umm …"

Jed winks. "Trust me, Mrs C. Trust me."

FORTY

I've only met Jed's big sister Saffron once before, at a family barbecue. While the rest of the family were nibbling on gourmet sausages topped with homemade sauce and wrapped in homemade olive bread, trying with all their might not to let anything fall on Jed's mum's freshly scrubbed patio, Saffron was tucking into a lentil burger, flicking gobs of tahini and chunks of eggplant carelessly all over the place. She offered palm and tarot card readings to any willing takers, and free spontaneous renditions of Xavier Rudd songs as well. All the while, her two sons—Miracle and Gift—danced naked around Jed's mum's bemused corgi, chanting Buddhist mantras.

The only time I saw her stop smiling the whole time was when her mum called her "Caroline". "It may be on my birth certificate, Maureen," Saffron said, "but that's just a piece of paper. Now peace the fuck out."

Jed's mum was mortified. I thought Saffron may well be the coolest person I'd ever met.

Saffron lives in Nimbin, so Jed's parents don't see her often. Which is, I think, exactly how they like it. She is back for the holidays, though, and we are going to visit.

"She's not staying with your family?" Mum asks Jed as we pile into Dad's vintage VK Commodore (the same car Warnie drives). It's a bit squishy in the back seat; my left knee is pressed against Jed's right one. My fingertips could brush his, if I wanted them to.

"Saffron says she doesn't believe in houses anymore," Jed says. "I think she just doesn't believe in *Mum's* house. Besides, I think Mum made it pretty clear she doesn't want a screaming baby keeping her up at all hours of the night. Not that I heard Courage cry once on Christmas day. She is freakishly happy. Guess you don't need a house to be happy. Just the wide open sky, circus skills, and tourists to pay for your henna tattoos."

"I'm so excited," Patience says. "I'm going to get a heart with 'Taylor' in it. For Taylor Swift," she explains when my dad looks at her quizzically.

He gives a heavy-hearted sigh. "And here was I thinking I'd raised two girls with intelligence and taste."

"Not everyone can be a connoisseur of fine music like you are, Steve," Jed says, smiling cheekily. "Your Twelfth Man cricket songs cassette collection is second to none."

"This is true," Dad says, laughing.

"Maybe you're right though, Dad," Patience says, looking pensive. "Maybe I should get something scientific instead. Like a DNA string or a chemical symbol. How can I decide? My two great loves! Taylor and science. How can I choose between them?" She flings her arms in the air, exhaling. "What are you going to get, Connie?" she asks.

I've been thinking about it. After Jed had explained what we were doing—and that it didn't involve permanent body art—I tossed a few ideas around in my head.

At first, I thought I might get "MOADM", as a celebration of joining the band. But then I thought that was a bit tame. If I am going to get a tattoo that would only last a couple of weeks, I might as well get something crazy, right?

Yep, it seems the old Connie is coming back. Constance would never have wanted to get a crazy tattoo. She would have refused to do this at all, because Viggo *definitely* doesn't approve of any form of body modification.

But *Connie* has always wanted a tattoo. And, who knows? Maybe one day soon she will get a real one.

After all, Viggo is gone for good, isn't he?

I don't need his approval for anything anymore.

Despite my broken heart, that knowledge feels kind of … liberating.

"I'm going to get Beezus in a heart," I declare. "After all, he is the only man in my life now."

"What am I, chopped liver?" asks my dad, smiling at me in the rear-view mirror.

"I so never understood that expression," I say. I turn to Jed. "Did you—" I realise he's looking at his lap, jaw clenched. "What's up, compadre?" I ask. "Having trouble deciding between Iron Maiden's Eddie and Megadeth's Vic Rattlehead for your tattoo?"

"Yeah. That's it," he says.

"Jed, tell Mum and Dad how awesome Connie was in MOADM," Patience says cheerily, not picking up on the black vibes emanating from Jed.

I'm worried, though. What is up with him? Jed is the least aggro metalhead in the world, usually, but his face is so stormy it reminds me …

I swallow.

It reminds me of Viggo.

And that memory makes me feel queasy.

It makes me think of the party. And … and the next memory.

FORTY-ONE

Memory 21

I was meant to be going with Jed to see a new fantasy epic at the cinema. But that was before Viggo decided the Landcare group wasn't meeting its KPIs and we needed an emergency working bee.

I hadn't hung out with Jed for ages. I still felt bad for ditching our East Coast trip, and I'd been forced to refuse almost every one of his invitations since. Viggo tied up every free moment with activities and study. But I'd promised Jed the cinema date. I'd promised I wouldn't bail.

Then Viggo suggested the working bee.

Of course, at the thought of missing out on a rare day away from school, the other members of the group groaned and protested.

"Constance, back me up here," Viggo said tetchily. "The student-free day is the most sensible day to do this, isn't it? Constance?"

I was looking down at my hands.

"Constance?"

I cleared my throat. "Um, well, Viggo ... we don't get that many days off, especially this time of year, what with midyear exams coming up and maybe ... I don't know ... There was a segment on Sunrise the other day about how it's really important that students have school and study free *days in the lead-up to exams, for mental health reasons, to, um, ease stress, which could hamper exam performance and stuff … and, so, maybe we should just …"*

I was sweating.

Viggo was looking at me as if I was a cockroach, a slug, something he wished very much to be able to squish under the toe of his handcrafted Salvatore Ferragamo boat shoe.

"Um …" I cleared my throat. "Maybe we should see if we could have some time off school on another day to do it. Instead of using our day off?"

Viggo was seething. His jaw was taut. There was a vein pulsing in his forehead. His fingers were gripping his pencil so hard I thought it might snap at any second.

I wanted to run from the room. My heart felt like it would burst from my chest. But I stayed, twisting my fingers, my cheeks burning.

"Right," Viggo said quietly. His quiet voice was—I'd discovered— much more frightening than when he yelled. He'd done that—yelled—once or twice, when I'd really stuffed up. Yelling meant he was frustrated. His quiet voice meant he was really, truly furious. He looked away from me around the table. "Well, that's Connie's opinion. Luckily, Connie's opinion doesn't count for much. Kacey, what do you think?"

Kacey flicked her long blond hair over her shoulder. "Obviously, I think Connie has a point," she said brightly. She smiled at me sympathetically. "But I also agree with you, Viggo. We shouldn't ask for time off. It would make us seem like we're only doing the Landcare group to get out of school instead of because of our passion for the environment. If we're really committed to this, we should use the student-free day. Besides, the weather forecast said it's going to be a super sunny day on Tuesday. So we could bring our bikinis and go for a swim when we're done! So … it might be okay—like a day off, anyway, Connie?" She smiled at me again. But Viggo only had eyes for her.

Viggo laughed. "Well, I don't own a bikini, Kacey …"

She rolled her eyes. "But I bet you have some boardies, don't you?"

Viggo leaned forwards. "As a matter of fact, I do own a pair of Ralph Lauren swimming shorts. I've been meaning to test them out."

My stomach flipped. If I didn't know that Viggo found Kacey shallow and dull—and that he was committed to me—I would have thought he was flirting with her.

But I knew he wasn't. Not really. He was just angry at me and was punishing me by being extra nice to Kacey. It was okay. I deserved it.

But I still felt like scum.

Viggo peered at me, his mouth set in a thin line. I knew I was going to get yelled at, big time, as soon as we were alone.

And Jed would be mad at me, because I would have to tell him I couldn't go to movies.

How did I always manage to stuff things up so badly?

"I think I'll actually get a wolf, like from the Sonata Arctica album covers." Jed's voice snaps me back to the present. "I'll save Eddie or Vic for when I get a real tattoo. I'm listening to Sonata a lot at the moment, so it makes sense that I get a tattoo reflecting that."

"I like Sonata," I say tentatively, and I'm pleased when he smiles.

"I know you do, Connie. You have great taste."

I feel myself blushing at the compliment. Jed always knows how to make me feel good about myself.

"Well, I'm getting the Australian cricket team logo," Dad grumbles. "With a big cross through it."

"I want a butterfly," Mum says wistfully. "I always thought if I got a real tattoo I'd get a butterfly."

"Is Saffron going to be able to do all these?" I ask Jed.

"Yeah. She's awesome."

"Runs in the family," I say.

Jed reaches over and takes my hand. Squeezes it.

It feels nice.

FORTY-TWO

As our henna dries, we sit outside Saffron's tent in the camping ground. We cradle mugs of hot, milky chai tea, which she made from scratch on the campfire stove.

"I'm glad you came over, Jed," she says. "We missed you yesterday. And I'm glad you brought Connie-girl. It's been far too long, little sister!"

My chest fills with warmth.

"Mum and Dad were saying they missed you too, Connie-girl. They said it's been ages since you came to visit. When they heard I was catching up with you today—"

"Wait," Jed interrupts, his face stricken. "You told them you were meeting us? Me? Were they … are they …"

"Completely furious?" Saffron grins. "Of course they are. You know Mum and Dad. They were so unchill that you bailed during the Buble-a-thon and didn't join us for the traditional eggnog, charades and Queen's Message evening. Well, they were until I spiked their eggnog. Then Mum suggested we change the game to strip charades and Dad said the Queen reminded him of a bulldog with a wig on. It was the best Christmas ever."

"So they're not going to …" Jed gulps. "When I get home, it'll be okay?"

"I'll come with you," Saffron promises. "I'll make it okay. And Connie should come too. You know they'll be fine with anything as long as Connie's involved."

"They really like me that much?" I ask softly.

Another memory flashes into my head—one I didn't tell Beezus—of the first time I met Viggo's parents.

FORTY-THREE

Memory 22

It was October. I'd wanted to meet Mr and Mrs MacDuff for … well, we'd been together since my birthday, just before Christmas. So I'd hoped to meet them for at least ten months.

Viggo always seemed to invite me over when they were out to dinner, or at work. Or on holidays in the Seychelles.

I'd asked, a couple of times, tentatively, if they might like to meet me. Viggo had blown me off. "Of course. But, you know, they're busy …"

I'd let it drop. And months went by.

And then …

I don't know what got into me. I knew that Viggo hated doing things he hadn't planned. He had his schedule honed to perfection and he became intensely grouchy if it got out of whack.

But I was excited—the Bangarra bookshop had shelved their copies of a new political memoir Viggo was coveting, a couple of days earlier than it was due out. I just happened to be in the shop—gazing wistfully at a Patrick Rothfuss I knew I'd never have time to read—when I saw the memoir on the new release stand. I knew Viggo was desperate to read it, so

I bought a copy and asked Dad if we could stop off at Viggo's on the way home.

"Of course," he said. "But I do have to go home straight away. Australia and the Windies are on the telly …"

"It's fine, Dad," I said. "Just drop me off. I'm sure Viggo and I will end up spending the afternoon together. I'll ask him to walk me home after, or I'll catch a bus."

"He bloody better walk you home," Dad said. "No daughter of mine is getting sent home from her boyfriend's house on public transport."

"He might have plans …" I protested.

Dad shook his head. "No plans are more important than my little girl. Jed always walks you home."

"Jed's not my boyfriend!"

"More's the pity," Dad muttered.

Then, I thought he was being sarcastic.

"Remember," Dad called as I bounced out of the car, "he walks you home. You deserve nothing less. Don't let him make you feel otherwise."

And I called back, "He makes me feel amazing."

Dad nodded. As I remember it now, though, he didn't look completely convinced.

But, at the time, all I cared about was getting to Viggo and giving him his book.

FORTY-FOUR

Memory 23

I raced up the steps and flung open the front door.

Again, I don't know what came over me. I always, always, always rang the bell. Even after ten months. I'd been letting myself into Jed's house since a couple of weeks after we met. His parents never batted an eyelid, even as I helped myself to a handful of his mum's fancy homemade biscuits and switched on the telly to MTV.

Maybe, in my excitement, I'd imagined I was at Jed's house instead of Viggo's. Maybe I really didn't think anything of letting myself in.

He was my boyfriend, after all. My boyfriend of ten months. Surely it was normal to treat his house as my own.

At least, that's what I thought until I heard his fury.

"Constance! What in heaven's name are you doing?"

I stopped dead in the middle of the MacDuff foyer.

I was facing not only Viggo, but his sister, Catherine, and a man and a woman.

Viggo's dad had thick, blond hair like Viggo's, and dark tanned skin. He looked much younger than I knew he must be. He had Viggo's long, straight nose and strong chin.

Viggo's mum was equally striking, with the piercing sea-green eyes that Viggo had inherited, long, shiny, chestnut-brown hair tied back in a sleek ponytail, and flawless peaches-and-cream skin. She wore a tight white tank and a short, white, pleated skirt, with a soft woollen cardigan tied around her shoulders.

Viggo's dad was all in white, too—shorts and a polo—and so were Viggo and Catherine. They were all holding white tennis racquets.

"I'm—I'm sorry. I'm interrupting." I backed towards the door.

"Viggo, who is this person?" Viggo's mum asked, a tight smile not quite reaching her eyes.

"A girl from school," Viggo said dismissively. It felt as if someone had shot an arrow through my heart.

A girl from school? I was his girlfriend. Why was he pretending I wasn't?

"Her name is Constance," he said. "I have no idea why she is here unannounced, but I'm certain she will understand we are just leaving …"

"Viggo …" Catherine looked at her brother accusingly. She knew I was more than just "a girl from school". We'd been on shopping trips together! She'd taken me to posh cafes! Catherine knew me. She'd stand up for me! "It's obvious the girl has something for you," she went on serenely. She raised a perfectly on-fleek eyebrow at me, as if in warning. "That must be why she burst in here so rudely. It must be important for her to have done so. Hear her out."

"I … I um—" I stammered. My face was burning. "I do … I have … here." I thrust the book into Viggo's hands and then turned and ran from the house.

I expected him to follow me.

I expected him to call my name and catch up to me and pull me into his arms and apologise—give me a really good reason for why he had just denied my existence in front of his parents.

He didn't follow me.

He didn't call my name.

And I just kept running, down his garden path, down his street, past the bus stop and all the way home.

"My parents adore you," Saffron says. "You know, they always hoped you and Jeremy would get married."

"Shut up, *Caroline*," Jed growls.

"Oh, come on, Lil Bro," Saffron says. "You know it's true." She puts an arm around me. "Seriously, Connie-girl. You could get away with murder with those two. How do you think my parents would have reacted if I had dyed my hair all kinds of crazy colours and dressed like a member of Pussy Riot when I was sixteen?"

"I'm going more for Four Non-Blondes," I say, grinning. "But I'll pay that. And are you telling me you weren't a rebel when you were sixteen, Saff? Because I seem to remember a certain dreadlocks incident ..."

"I grew them for six months," Saffron says wistfully. "I hid them by tying my hair back and wearing sun hats. But Mum cottoned on eventually ..."

"And made you cut them off," I finished. "The bob suited you though."

"It wasn't a bob. It was a bowl cut," Saffron protests. "I looked like an extra from *Oliver*. But you see my point? I grew dreadlocks and as punishment I got a bad haircut and a month's grounding. You could turn up at our place dressed like Jack Sparrow and Mum would say your new look suited you. When I moved to Nimbin, I think she was relieved. But then you disappeared too and she was devastated."

"I didn't disappear!" I protest.

"You did. Mum told me. You went to Viggo-land."

I look at my family for support.

I don't find it.

"It's true," my mum says, shrugging. "When you took up with that boy—"

"He's not 'that boy'! He's Viggo!"

Mum ignores me. "You did disappear. Your life became all about him. And you became the girl he wanted you to be. You changed so completely, Connie. We were all worried about you. In fact, if you and Viggo hadn't broken up—thank God—your father and I were going to stage an intervention."

I look at Mum, open-mouthed. "A … what now?"

"We were going to try and convince you how toxic your relationship was." Now I'm staring at Dad. *Toxic relationship?* Since when had my father started reading *Cleo*?

"Your father has been devouring every parenting book he could get his hands on, trying to come up with a solution to this," Mum explains. "We both have. We were desperate for a way to fix you."

"*Fix* me?" I gasp. "But I'm not … broken."

Mum's voice is gentle. "The only one who couldn't see it was you. Jed agreed with us. He offered to help us. We called him Christmas Day and—"

"Wait." I hold up my hands. "You *called him Christmas Day*?" I turn to Jed. "You only came over because Mum and Dad asked you to? You wouldn't have come otherwise? And, so, what is all this? The memory stuff? The adventures? Is this all something Mum and Dad asked you to do, because they read it in a parenting book?"

Jed looks stricken. "No, Connie! I wanted to see you. I wanted to hang out with you. I've been wanting to hang out with you this whole past year, but you've been too busy with Viggo …"

"Because God forbid I should be happy!" I cry, throwing my hands in the air. "God forbid I should like someone and be liked back and try and make myself into a better version of me. I can't just stay the way I was because that's how you liked me." I look at Jed and Mum and Dad as I say this.

"And besides," I say to Mum and Dad, "you were always

making fun of my hair and my clothes and my music. So I changed and then you didn't like me that way, either." Tears are running down my face now. "I changed and I thought you'd be happy. I thought Viggo would be happy. The only person I knew wouldn't be happy was Jed, but that didn't matter, somehow, because the way I was before he never liked me as much as I wanted him to, anyway …"

The words are flying out of me, but it feels as if my brain's not in charge. I never really thought these things, did I? I never really thought Mum and Dad didn't like me. I never really thought that Jed didn't like me … enough for *what?*

He is my best friend. That's all he is.

What do I mean he doesn't like me *enough?*

"Connie …" Mum grabs my hand. "Connie, you know none of that is true. Your father and I adore you, crazy hair and clothes and music and all. We teased you, but it was only in fun, same as we tease Patty for loving Taylor Swift. We love every little thing about you. I have no idea where this is coming from."

"We are so proud of everything about you, Connie!" Dad says, ruffling my hair. "We even grew to love your music. Although Ben Folds is not a patch on Jimmy Buffett. Or the Twelfth Man." He winks at Jed. "But he's not bad. I've been listening to old Foldsy a lot, lately, since you haven't been listening to him as much. I've missed him. Connie, you're perfect, just as you are. And if we thought you really wanted to have boring hair and wear those boring suits and listen to boring classical music, we would have loved that about you too, but we never really believed you wanted it. We always knew you were just doing it for that boy and—"

"What do you mean I never liked you enough?" Jed interrupts.

I turn away from Dad. Everyone else fades away and all I can see is him.

My Jed.

With his ridiculously long hair and big nose and dark, intense eyes.

Staring at me.

And I think it again. *You never liked me enough. Not as much as I wanted you to.*

The thought scares me. So I push it away.

"Of course you didn't like me enough," I snap. "You didn't like me enough to come over when you first found out Viggo and I broke up. You didn't like me enough to even stay at my party longer than five minutes this year, because it wasn't cool or 'metal' enough for you. If you'd stayed, you would have been there when Viggo and I … You would have been there to … But instead, you show up two days later, only because my parents ask you to. Some best friend. You *don't* like me enough, Jed. You came to my party, got with some girl—" a pain goes through my chest as I say this, "and you left without even saying goodbye and when —when it happened … I came looking for you and you weren't there. And the next day, when I needed you to come and make me feel better, you weren't there and—"

"You weren't there for a year, Connie," Jed says. He's standing up. "For a whole year you had no idea what was going on in my life. You had no idea I joined the band. You had no idea Meg got a job. You had no idea my dad *lost* his job and is now working at a call centre while he looks for something better. You had no idea that two—*two*—girls asked me out but I said no to both of them. You had no idea I came—" he holds two fingers close together, as if he's about to pinch me, "—this close to failing maths. You had no idea I got *pneumonia,* for Pete's sake. I was off school for two weeks and you didn't even notice. *And* you had no idea I came to loathe, loathe, *loathe* Viggo MacDuff. And all because you were so fricking obsessed with the guy. You couldn't see what an arsehole he actually is—sorry, Patience and Chase parents."

My mum and dad nod dumbly. Patience says, "I said douchebag before. It's okay."

"You said what?" Mum asks.

"Later," says Patience. "You were saying?" she asks Jed.

He shakes his head. "Or maybe you could see what a shit person he is and you stayed with him anyway. I don't know. What I do know is, in this past year I've lost all respect for *Constance* Chase. Connie Chase was my best friend. The *clone* you became when you took up with MacDick isn't her. And when your parents called to tell me you were upset and they thought it might be something to do with Viggo, yeah, I did think 'hurray', because I hoped you'd broken up. I did pray to the gods of metal that that was the case. I hoped, actually, that you'd done something really bad to piss Viggo off. I hoped you'd broken that motherfu—" He glances at Mum and Dad. "Sorry."

"It's fine," Dad says, and he sounds like he means it.

"I hoped you'd broke his heart. But I called him and you know what he said? He said, 'I don't care, Jeremy. She never meant anything to me anyway. She was a project. But then she started to really *irritate* me. She didn't know how to keep in her place.'"

"That motherfu—"

"Steve!" my mum gasps, whacking Dad on the arm.

My face is burning. My throat feels scratchy and my belly feels hollow. "He really said that?" I whisper. "You're not just saying that to make me … to make me …"

"What? Despise him like I do?" Jed shakes his head. "I was hoping you'd come to do that all by yourself but, it seems, you're not as clever as I thought you were. You're not the person I thought you were at all, Connie. You might have the skate shoes back on. You might have wicked blue hair. But you still *want* to be Viggo's 'Constance'. And if he walked back in here right now, you'd go back to him in a second, wouldn't you?"

"No, she wouldn't!" Patience declares. She looks at me, eyes wide and questioning. "Would you, Connie?"

"I ..."

"Forget it. You don't have to answer." Jed begins to back away. "I'm just going to head off. I got a text from Leah asking if I want to catch up and ... you know what? I think I do. See you back at home later, Saff. See you, Patience. Bye, Steve—good luck with the rest of the test. Thanks for coming out, Lesley. Hope you had fun."

And then he turns and walks away.

He doesn't even say goodbye.

And, for some reason, my heart aches worse now than it ever has before.

FORTY-FIVE

Memory 24

It was the Monday after my humiliation at Viggo's house.

I was loitering by his locker. I did this every day. I arrived early so I could be there waiting for him, with a long black coffee and a cheese and alfalfa sandwich on soy and pumpkin seed bread. I made it for him at home before school. It was his favourite breakfast. Viggo ran five kilometres on his treadmill and then crammed in an hour of study before showering and heading to school. He never had time for breakfast.

He didn't ask me to bring him breakfast. I volunteered.

This was the first morning Viggo had ever been late.

He didn't apologise or offer any explanation. All he said was, "Excuse me, Connie. I'm in a hurry and you're in my way."

"Oh. Sorry." I moved away from his locker. "Um, do you want your breakfast?"

He shook his head. "No time." He pulled books from his locker, scooping them into a pile in his arms. When he was finished, he turned and made to move away without another word to me.

"Viggo!" I called after him.

He paused and looked back over his shoulder, his lips pursed. "If you don't mind, I'm running rather behind here."

"Um, sorry, it's just … if this is about you being mad because I showed up at your house yesterday …"

"What's 'this'?" he snapped, his fingers making inverted commas in the air. "There is no 'this'. I am simply late to class. So if you don't mind—"

Just then, Kacey Kuusela rounded the corner into the hallway. "Hi, Viggo," she said. She looked past him to me. "Hi, Connie. You look gorgeous today. I told you that shirt would suit you! Organic hemp is super-great, isn't it? I'm so glad more designers are working with it!"

"Yeah, thanks," I said distractedly. I still wasn't quite used to Kacey being nice to me, but today I was much more concerned with what was going on with Viggo.

"Viggo, have you got a minute?" Kacey asked, her forehead creasing. "I need to talk to you about … um, Landcare stuff."

"Of course," Viggo said, without another look in my direction.

This was November. Viggo and I had been together for eleven and a half months. And I felt as if I was a piece of rubbish beneath his Ferragamo heel.

I took a sip on Viggo's coffee and gagged. It was horrible. He'd never let me share it before, and we'd never actually gone to a café together …

For the first time, this struck me as not only strange but wrong. We'd been together nearly a year and, apart from that first meal at Ronaldo's (when we weren't even a couple yet), Viggo hadn't once taken me out on one coffee date, let alone another dinner.

That wasn't right, was it?

I reasoned that we were always busy. I told myself I was lucky Viggo made time for me at all in his busy schedule. I should be grateful I got to take up some of his time, most days.

But still. A romantic dinner wouldn't go astray.

Maybe for my birthday? Our anniversary?

He'd have to take me out then, wouldn't he?

I went to throw the sandwich and coffee in a bin, before catching myself.

To do that would be completely wasteful, not to mention terrible for the environment. Plus, I'd put a lot of effort into that sandwich.

A girl I recognised from one of Viggo's clubs—World War One History, perhaps?—averted her eyes as she approached.

"Hey?" I said.

She jerked and looked at me, startled, deer-in-headlights. "Are you talking to me?" she squeaked.

"Um, yes?" She was still staring. "You're in the World War One group, right?

The girl shook her head. "American ... Civil War." She cleared her throat three times. Her face was the colour of beetroot. And then I realised. She was ... nervous? About speaking to me?

"Oh, right," I said. "Um, well, I know we haven't talked before, really, but my name's Connie—Constance—and—"

"I know who you are," she said shyly. "You're Viggo MacDuff's girlfriend."

"I'm Connie," I repeated.

"Yes," she said again, dragging the word out, as if she thought I was a little bit slow. "Viggo MacDuff's girlfriend."

I felt strangely deflated. Usually, being known as Viggo's girlfriend made me happy, but just for once I thought it might be nice to be known as more than just that. To be known as Connie Chase, who was ...

An unsettling thought wrapped around me. What am I if I'm not Viggo MacDuff's girlfriend?

I shook myself. I was just tired. I'd stayed up too late transcribing Viggo's notes on Mayor of Casterbridge. I tried a smile. "Yeah, that's me. Would you like a sandwich?"

She hesitated, peering at me as if I was crazy. I hadn't been looked at like that since Jed and I dressed up for Costume Day as the "Empty Children" from Doctor Who. Gas masks and all. We thought we looked awesome but we made a few people scream ...

"It's Viggo's favourite," I added wearily.

Her eyes brightened. "Viggo eats these sandwiches? Do you think that's why he's so smart and great and stuff?"

"Yeah," I said dryly. "That's it. It's the sandwich."

The girl snatched the parcel from my hand. "Thanks." She shoved the sandwich into her mouth. "You're so lucky," she said through a mouthful of brown dough. "Viggo MacDuff is the greatest. And you—"

She paused, her brain seeming to catch up with her mouth.

"I'm what?" I prompted, pretty sure I knew what she was going to say.

"Well, you know what everyone says," she said, shrugging.

"No. I don't know."

A wicked look spread across her face. "Everyone says that Viggo picked you to be his girlfriend because he knew you'd make the perfect personal assistant."

"What?" I gasped. "I'm not Viggo's PA. I'm his girlfriend."

The girl looked pointedly at the sandwich. "Mm hmm," she said, and then walked away.

"I'm not Viggo's personal—" I muttered to myself, just as an alarm went off on my phone. I pulled it out of my pocket. "Don't forget to clean out Viggo's locker," it said.

I grimaced. I had forgotten. Viggo had been complaining on Friday that his locker had become so crammed with books he couldn't find anything. I'd offered to clean it out for him. He hadn't asked me to do it. I'd offered.

But still … Was it wrong that I offered? What sort of girlfriend volunteered to clean out her boyfriend's rubbish?

The bell rang for Home Group.

I looked at Viggo's locker. I remembered how grateful he'd seemed when I said I'd clean it for him. I thought of how disappointed he'd be if I didn't do it.

"I'll do it at recess," I muttered to myself. Viggo had a meeting then anyway. I began to walk to class. "I am Viggo MacDuff's girlfriend," I whispered, trying to make myself feel better. It usually worked, reminding myself of that.

But now a voice inside my head insisted: You are Viggo MacDuff's personal assistant.

"*Shut up,*" I whispered to the voice. "*And, even if I am, being Viggo's PA is ten times better than just being plain old Connie Chase.*"

I pull myself out of my memory.

Dad and Saffron are discussing cricket, while Saffron breast-feeds Courage. Mum and Patience are playing on the floor with Gift and Miracle.

Jed is gone.

And I ... I am plain old Connie Chase. And now I don't even have Jed to make me feel better. I am all alone.

FORTY-SIX

Back at home, I shower and dress in clean clothes. I have to hunt around in my wardrobe to find clothes that aren't *Constance*. I discover, stuffed in a bin bag, a bunch of my old tee-shirts, including one Jed had made for me a couple of years back.

"You're the magic that holds the sky up from the ground." It's from a Ben Folds' song, of course. One of my favourites. "Magic".

It smells like dust, but I pull it over my head anyway. It's comfortable. None of my "Viggo" clothes feel comfortable.

With a pang in my belly I realise this shirt feels like Jed. It feels like safety and comfort and home. And magic.

I slump down at my desk. Beezus nips at my feet. I let my eyes drift over the piles of books that litter the table in front of me. School books and books Viggo has lent me.

I guess I'll have to get those back to him. Somehow.

And then I see it. The parcel. *"Merry Christmas, Mr Sardick."*

I cringe. It's my present from Jed. Jed, my best friend. Jed, the boy I've neglected for a whole year while I've been busy being "Viggo MacDuff's girlfriend".

Jed who continued hanging out with Viggo, even though he hated him.

Jed, whose parents hoped we'd get married …

My belly does that twisting thing again. I close my eyes and, for the first time since Viggo came into my life, it isn't his face I see.

Jed's dark coal eyes. Jed's long dark hair. Jed's funny big nose.

The way he only ever smiles with one side of his mouth. The way he twists his hair when he's nervous. The way he pats Tallulah fondly as he walks around to the driver's side, even though the stupid car barely ever works. The way he cuddles Beezus. The way his eyes sparkle when he's telling me about a new musical discovery.

Jed, whose parents always hoped we'd get married.

Jed, who left his family on Christmas Day to be with me.

He wouldn't do that just because my parents asked him to. Or just because his family were playing Michael Buble. I know Jed. I know he might act the tough guy, and his perfect parents might annoy the hell out of him, but he loves them to bits and he does get a kick out of Christmas with them, despite the twee-ness of it all. He's told me so before. He likes his mum's perfect roast. He likes the fancy Christmas crackers she buys. He likes his family hanging out together, just being happy.

Jed loves his family Christmas. And yet he ditched it for me. And I hadn't even batted an eyelid. I hadn't questioned his motives, or suggested he should go back. I just, selfishly, let him stay; let him comfort me; let him take me on all these adventures as he tried to make me see that …

What?

Why had he done it?

And, suddenly, I know.

Jed took me on all those adventures to make me see that I could do fun things without Viggo; that I could *be* fun without Viggo.

That I could be *Connie* without Viggo.

Connie-girl.

His Connie-girl.

I pick up the present. As soon as I do I know I was wrong thinking it was a CD. It's too heavy, and too rectangular, not square and lightweight like a CD is. I carefully unstick the tape, noticing for the first time, too, that the gift is carefully wrapped, as if Jed had taken time to get it right.

"Oh," I moan, pressing the present to my chest as the paper falls to the floor.

Jed hasn't given me a CD, or a book about one of his favourite metal acts, or even a joke present like he sometimes gave me—a fake moustache or a Britney Spears poster.

He's given me a photo, in an expensive-looking frame.

A photo that I know was taken not long before Viggo arrived in Bangarra.

A photo of me and Jed.

We are on the beach. There is a sunrise behind us. We look exhausted and I remember why. We'd been up all night. We'd snuck into the wildlife park not far from our houses and spent the night with the animals.

It was Jed's idea, because I'd complained that whenever we went to the park all the best animals were asleep. The devils and bats and quolls—the nocturnal animals—didn't show their faces during the daytime, and they were the animals I wanted to see.

So Jed suggested we climb the fence and pay a visit to those animals when it wasn't sleepy time.

We sat, cuddled up against the cold, watching the small marsupials play and feed and conduct their secret, nighttime lives under a starry sky. Jed kissed my hair and thanked me for wishing to do this; wishing to see the animals. He thanked me for including him on my adventures.

"You're way overtired," I whispered back. "It's making you soppy."

"Nah, it's the full moon," he replied. "Like Sonata Arctica say. It's making me crazy. I'll start turning werewolf any second."

I remembered the song. I liked it. I sang a couple of bars. *"You should have locked the open door. Run away, run away, run away. Full moon is on the sky and he's not a man anymore."*

"You know the words." Jed's voice was gentle. "You know, I know all the words to all of your songs, too. I know everything. I remember everything."

"That's why you're my best friend," I replied, and we lapsed into contented silence.

As the light turned from jet black to grey, we sneaked out again and ran, holding hands, to the beach, where we asked the first jogger who came by to take our picture. "So we can remember this forever," Jed said, and I looked at him quizzically.

"Why remember this?" I asked. "We've done weird and crazy stuff like this heaps of times before and you haven't required a photographic memento.

Jed shrugged. "It was the night I found out you knew all the words to the Sonata song."

"And that means something?"

"That means everything."

In the photograph, my pink-streaked hair is a bird's nest. My tee-shirt—the same one I'm wearing now—is crumpled. My jeans are dirty from crawling around on my knees in the wildlife park. Viggo would be disgusted.

But, as I smile for the camera, I look blissful.

But it's not the expression on my face that brings tears to my eyes.

Jed isn't looking at the camera at all. He's looking at me. And the look on *his* face ...

"He loves you."

I turn around. Patience is leaning on my door frame. "You know that, right? That boy loves the shit out of you."

I don't even think to tell her off for swearing again. I just nod. "I think I know that now."

"And he's awesome. So much better than that Viggo … bad person. I wanted you to get together with him all along."

"Too late now," I mumble, dropping the photograph on my bed. "I took him for granted and ignored him when he needed me and then he got with another girl at my party and he's on a date with her now and besides …"

"Besides what? And if you tell me you still love Viggo MacDuff—"

"No."

It's out of my mouth before I have time to think about it; before I have time to question whether or not it's true.

Is it true?

Have I stopped loving Viggo?

"Good," Patience says emphatically. "Because I saw your ribs, and if they're like that for the reason I think they are … If those marks are there for the reason I *think* they are …"

I shake my head. "You don't understand, Patience. It was my fault."

"Try me," she says through gritted teeth.

I shake my head. "That's the one memory I'm not telling."

"Fine." Patience reaches across me and snatches Beezus into her arms. "But you're not getting your ferret back until you do."

"Patty—" I protest wearily.

She's halfway out the door before she turns. "You can *not* tell me if you don't want to. But I want you to tell Jed."

"He's on a *date*," I protest.

"Connie, he ditched Christmas to be with you. I think he'll ditch a date."

"Patty, you are the best sister, you know that?" I say.

Patience nods. "I know. You're still not getting your ferret back. He's coming with me to watch Dr Brian Cox. Oh and, by the way, Em called, like, a million times. Mum has been putting her off, saying you're sick and you're not up to talking—because we figured you weren't—but she says Em is getting increasingly manic and she's threatening to fly home from Queensland tonight if you don't talk to her. So you might want to buzz her, okay?"

"Okay." I flop down on my bed as my bedroom door clicks shut, Patience and Beezus on the other side of it.

I pick up my phone. I thought, vaguely, that I heard the bouncy sounds of "Underground", Ben Folds Five's ode to weird and crazy. Jed must have changed my ringtone to that from the old one, which was a tribute to Viggo. Sure enough, when I unlock the screen, it tells me I've had twenty missed calls. All from Em.

What the heck is going on with her? I mean, sure, I know I said I'd call back, but this is going a bit far, isn't it? I press the green handset button to return the call.

"You have reached the message bank of—" The electronic voice begins, and then it switches to Em's sunny tone. "Emily Chambers. Please leave a message after the tone ..."

The message bank beep sounds. "Em. Hi. It's Connie. Sorry, I know you've been trying to get hold of me because I didn't call you back. I'm sorry. I've been kind of busy. Um, I'll try you again later."

I hang up and put down my phone. Suddenly, I'm overcome by overwhelming tiredness. I lay my head down on my pillow.

I don't remember anything else that day.

FORTY-SEVEN

I'm woken by the smell of blueberries.

I prise my eyes open. They feel like sandpaper. The light in my room is bright. Not dawning bright; halfway-through-the-morning bright. I'm stiff and I'm cold from sleeping on top of the covers all night. I'm still in my clothes. My unbrushed teeth are coated in fuzz.

I look to the side. Patience is sitting by my bed, with Beezus on her knee and a plate piled high with blueberry pancakes in her outstretched hand.

"I decided to forgive you," she says. "Because a) Beezus missed you last night. He pined for hours. And pining for him seems to involve trying to eat my toes. And also, because b) I figured if *he* could forgive you, then I had no excuse."

"He?"

Patience indicates with her head towards my open door. Jed is leaning in the doorway. He looks … strange, somehow. It takes me a moment to realise why.

He's not wearing black.

He's dressed in a pale blue shirt and tie and clean blue jeans, and his hair is confined in a ponytail. He's clean-shaven, too. The five o'clock shadow is gone, and so is the little triangle-shaped goatee from his chin.

He looks nice. Not quite like the Jed I know and—my thoughts stumble on the word—love, but nice.

"What are you doing here so early?" I croak.

"It's eleven am," he says, smiling. "I thought you'd be awake. But I showed up to find Patience cooking you breakfast and you— Lady Muck—nowhere to be seen."

"I feel like muck," I admit. I sit up. "Jed, I'm sorry about—"

"I'll leave you guys to it," Patience says quietly and with a little smile. She puts Beezus on the floor and the pancake plate on my bedside table. "I'm going back to Saffron's tent with Mum to have my cards read."

"You're thirteen," I say. "Why do you want to know the future? Isn't the pleasure of being thirteen in the not-knowing?"

"The pleasure's *always* in the not-knowing," she says sagely. "I don't *believe* in the cards. Mum and I just have to get out of the house because Australia is tanking and Dad's losing the plot. And plus I want to hang out with Gift and Miracle. Those little dudes are *cool*. I'm teaching them about quantum physics. See you tonight." She stops just before leaving the room. "Kiss him if he'll let you," she says cheekily before she disappears.

"Whoa." Jed tries to run his hand through his hair, but it catches. "Awkward."

"I know," I say, concentrating on getting upright and off the bed. "What's *she* on about? Crazy child." I reach for my pancakes and take a bite.

"They look really great," Jed says, "but would you mind not eating them all? I, um, we kind of have reservations."

My head jerks up. "Reservations? For breakfast?"

"It's now eleven-fifteen," Jed says. "Lunch."

"Oh. Um. Okay." I take another bite and reluctantly place the plate back on my desk. "But ... wait ... you had a date."

Jed looks away. "Did I say that?"

"You didn't *not* say that."

"I was angry," he says quietly. "Leah's nice. She's also a lesbian."

"Oh. Right."

"But we did hang out last night and it was fun. I'm sorry if I made it sound as if there was more to it. I was crabby at you. We watched *Star Wars* together. Her girlfriend is more of a *Star Trek* person. They fought about it. I took Leah's side and we bonded over a shared hatred of C3PO. That's it. I enjoyed hanging out with her, though, Connie. You would too. You should get to know her. You'd like her. And her friends. They're all nice. They like Pokemon. They play Magic cards, too. Now you're not with Viggo, you can do stuff like that again."

"Right."

"So anyway, I thought today we'd finish listening to your memories. We must be nearly at the end. But we won't do any more adventures. Instead, I thought we could do ... *nice* things. Things that bastard Viggo should have done with you. Like take you out for a fancy lunch."

"How did you ..." Jed raises an eyebrow. I puff out my cheeks. "I'll just shower and get dressed. I have a million 'Viggo' dresses I can wear."

Jed shakes his head. "Not a Viggo dress. A Connie dress."

"Oh. I don't have many of those."

"You have the one with the cherries on it," he says, ticking off on his fingers. "And the one with Hello Kitty. And the one with the polka dots and—"

"You really do remember everything," I say, looking at him in awe.

He blushes. "About you, Connie-girl, yes, I do."

FORTY-EIGHT

I pick the Hello Kitty dress, not because Jed likes it—though I know he does, since he helped me choose it from the Vinnies Retro Shop—but because *I* like it. It's fun. It's the opposite of every dress I've worn in the past year.

I wear it with my Vans and stripy knee-length socks. I rummage around in the back of my bathroom drawer and find the pot of sticky star-shaped glitter I'd shoved back there a year before, when Viggo told me it made me look "juvenile", and I carefully paste a few stars to the corners of my eyes.

I look up at the mirror and smile. I look like Connie again.

Well, almost.

I find my nail scissors in the drawer.

"Whoa," says Jed when I walk back in the room. "Your hair …"

"Is just the way I like it," I say, ruffling the short fringe I've just cut for myself—the fringe I spent a year growing out because Viggo considered fringes "juvenile". He likes it just past the shoulders, all one length, all one colour and long enough to be tied back into a practical ponytail with no clips or pins.

I have clips in my hair now. Two of them. Shaped like cherries.

And my hair is now grazing my jawline, cut jaggedly with my nail scissors.

And I have a completely juvenile fringe.

"I was wondering what was taking you so long," says Jed. His eyes are sweeping over me. He looks pleased with what he sees and I'm glad. I'm glad to make him happy. But it's not the most important thing. The most important thing is that I am happy.

The thought of it hits me like a revelation.

The most important thing is that I'm happy with myself.

When was I last happy with myself, without Viggo's approval?

When was I last happy with myself, full stop?

"I think I never really liked myself," I blurt to Jed. "Before Viggo. I think I always thought I was … a bit of a loser."

Jed nods slowly. "I know. I knew. You always used to talk yourself down. You called yourself fat and stupid and crazy. And I—"

"You always told me I was beautiful and clever and crazy," I say, laughing. "And that if my body was 'fat' then fat was awesome and beautiful. I never listened to you. I just kept believing the voices in my head. And then Viggo came along …"

"And he encouraged the voices," Jed says grimly. "Because it suited his purpose."

"And I let him." My head jerks up. "And you let me let him."

"I did try to tell you." Jed takes my hand and squeezes it. "Countless times. I asked you if you were happy with Viggo. I told you I thought you were changing and that I wasn't sure Viggo was good for you."

"I ignored you," I say, remembering now. "I thought Viggo was good for me."

"Are you …" I see Jed's Adam's Apple bob up and down as he swallows. "Do you feel differently now? After telling me the memories? Do you think maybe I was right? Do you think maybe Viggo wasn't so good for you after all? Have you stopped …"

He doesn't need to finish. I know what he's trying to say.

Have you stopped loving him?

I don't reply straight away. Because, truthfully, I don't know the answer. I thought I loved Viggo. I really did. I was swept up in his *greatness*. I was flattered that such a gorgeous, smart, popular, brilliant, "going-places" boy would want *me*.

But he didn't want me, really, did he? He wanted Constance.

And I'd thought, for a while, that was me.

I was Constance.

But then, as soon as we broke up, I put my sneakers back on. Without even thinking twice.

And the negative voices in my head didn't go away when I took up with Viggo. They just got louder. And the only person telling me the voices were wrong wasn't Viggo—my boyfriend—it was Jed. Still Jed. Always Jed.

Maybe I had loved Viggo. But he didn't love me. I know that now. Otherwise he wouldn't have encouraged me to hate myself.

Viggo didn't love me. But Jed …

"So, Leah's a lesbian?" I say quietly. "And you got asked out by those other girls but you said no …"

Jed lifts a shoulder. "I was waiting for a girl with mad, multi-coloured hair and Joe Cool Vans to come back from the planet she disappeared to."

"How … how long have you felt like this?" I realise I'm still holding his hand. I squeeze it tightly.

"Oh, well, there was a Pokemon party a few years back …" Jed's face is glowing. "But …" He clears his throat. "Connie, I don't know … This whole past year I've watched you with Viggo and it's broken my heart. Seriously. Watching you with that guy has been the hardest thing I've ever been through. And you did love him. I could see it. You were completely besotted. I don't think I can handle it if you go back to him."

"I'm not going back to him," I promise, and in that moment I know it's true. My hand moves to my ribs and I wince.

"Is it time to tell me the last memory?" Jed asks, his face stony.

"Not yet," I say. "Let's just have a nice lunch first, at a fancy restaurant. And the whole time we're there, let's not talk about Viggo MacDuff."

FORTY-NINE

L unch is wonderful.

But of course it is. Jed organised it. And Jed knows me better than anyone in the world.

Retro opened in the city not long before Viggo arrived. There were flyers up on the noticeboards at school and stuck to telegraph poles in Bangarra. It's a fifties' style rockabilly cafe, but its gimmick is a jukebox with music from the forties to the nineties.

And it has special days that celebrate particular decades. Sometimes, it has nineties' days.

Of course, I've been longing to go, but I never mentioned it to Viggo. I knew there was no point asking.

Jed asked me one day if I wanted to go with him. Viggo was there, though, so of course I said no.

But my heart ached.

Now, my heart is singing. It may be singing bad nineties' bubblegum pop, but it's singing.

"Stay there," says Jed as we pull up outside. He clambers out of Talullah and races around to my door and holds it open for me. Viggo *never* did that. Viggo never opened doors for me, never carried my bags, never pulled out my chair.

And I told myself it was because he was a feminist. Because he respected women. Because he considered us equal, not weaker.

And I ignored the voice in the back of my head that said, *You can't really be a feminist, Viggo. Because you don't like it when girls are loud. You don't like it when we're opinionated or confident. You want us to be seen and not heard. You don't open doors for us because you don't care enough to do it.*

I don't expect Jed to open my door. And I don't *need* him to. Women *are* more than capable of opening doors for themselves.

But sometimes the gesture is nice. Because it means someone cares.

"Thank you," I say softly as I step out of the car. Jed takes my hand.

"You're welcome," he says.

I can't help laughing. "Jed?"

His eyes are searching my face. "Yes?"

"Be a bit more metal," I say. "Be a bit more *Jed*."

Jed makes his hand into a "devil horns" salute. "Satan," he says, laughing. Then he shakes his head. "This is Jed," he says. "It's just fancy Jed. It's 'taking Connie out on a date' Jed."

A shiver runs up my spine. "Is that what this is?" I ask. "A date?"

Jed's face pales. "It can ... I mean, it's not ... it doesn't have to ... shit, sorry, Connie. I didn't think. I mean, you just broke up and ..."

I put my hand on his mouth. "It's fine," I say. "A date is fine."

And it is. I mean, sure, it feels weird—Jed is my best friend—but ... it feels right too.

Viggo felt *hard* and *scary* and *uncomfortable*.

Jed feels *right*.

"Let's go and have a date," I say.

"And then, afterwards, you can tell me the last memory."

I nod, ignoring the lump in my throat. I don't want to have to say it. I don't want to have to relive it.

But it happened. It's real.

And somehow I know that, when I tell it to Jed, that's when I'll start to make proper sense of it. It's only seeing it through Jed's eyes—and Patience's too—that has made me realise Viggo MacDuff isn't quite as awesome as I thought he was. Somehow I know it's only through telling that final memory to Jed that I'll know what actually happened that night at my party.

And then maybe, finally, I can let it go.

Maybe, finally, I can forget about Viggo MacDuff.

Maybe I can stop loving him.

I shiver again. Because I know, deep in my heart of hearts, that I do still love Viggo MacDuff, a little bit.

But I need to stop. I need to stop now. Because standing next to me is a long-haired metal fan who has always loved me just for me.

I take his hand. "Let's go and eat and sing along to Steps songs," I say.

"Maybe they'll play some nineties' Metallica," he says hopefully.

"Unlikely," I point out.

"Unlikely," he echoes. "But I don't really care. Because I'm here with you and that's all that matters."

FIFTY

Afterwards, we walk out into the afternoon light, with our bellies full of sushi and cappuccino and our ears full of an assortment of nineties' pop, indie rock and, yes, even some nineties' metal.

I'm feeling joyful. I had the best time, eating and laughing, and nattering to Jed about all the old crap we *used* to talk about. Music and movies and kids from school. And how *exactly* we're going to find a Tardis in Bangarra. Nothing *worthy*. Nothing *serious* or *important*. None of the stuff that Viggo and I would have discussed over lunch. Just fun stuff. But, somehow, it feels important. Because I'm talking about it with Jed. And it's *our* fun, silly stuff.

Jed-and-Connie stuff.

Coned stuff.

And I realise, as we're talking, that there was no Viggo-and-Connie stuff. No "Congo" stuff. There was only Viggo stuff.

Why the heck did I let myself disappear? Why did I become Constance?

I know why. Because Connie never felt good enough. But why didn't she feel good enough?

I ask Jed. "I have no idea," he says truthfully. "I told you how wonderful you are, all the time. So did your parents. And my parents. And Patience. I think …" He rubs his temples. "Connie, there's this organisation I've been reading about that helps geeks with depression …"

"You think I have depression?" I ask, ignoring the part about me being a geek. I am a geek. Or at least I was until a year ago.

Jed shrugs, pushing a chunk of sticky rice around his plate. "I don't know how else Viggo could have taken you over as thoroughly as he did," he says without looking at me. "And, also, there's more. I was remembering how—at primary school—Viggo used to get kids to do stuff for him. He'd pick the bullied kid, the sad kid, the awkward kid and he'd offer them friendship in exchange for … things. Services, I guess. Like getting his lunch or packing up his gear for him at the end of the day. Then, after a while, he'd get sick of them—they'd do something to annoy him or he'd just get tired of their company—and he'd move on to the next kid." He looks up. "I never realised until recently that *I* was one of those kids."

"But … you and Viggo stayed friends," I protest. "He didn't move on from you. And you weren't a sad kid … were you?"

Jed shrugs again. "I think I *was* a sad kid. Until I met you. And Viggo didn't have the opportunity to get sick of me, because he moved away. And I *kept* … providing services for him. I'd mail him over his favourite organic coffee beans that you can only buy at the Bangarra market, or articles he wanted from the local paper, or I'd provide him with gossip about people from primary school. I even emailed him the notes I took in class, so he could 'compare our educational institutions'." Jed rolls his eyes. "Yeah, right. I kept on being Viggo's servant. I never realised it, though. I just thought we were being friends. I should have noticed he never gave anything back. And I should have known by then, anyway, what real friendship is. Because I had it with you."

"Actual *crap*," I breathe. "He really is a Class A Space Pig. Thank you for finally making me realise that."

"I think maybe that was the easy part," Jed says. "The hard bit will be getting you to realise you're worth more than the way he treated you. The past year I've been able to work that out myself, but you were in deeper than I was. Viggo was just a childhood friend to me. He was your boyfriend. And I think the way you feel about yourself goes much further than Viggo MacDuff."

I don't say anything. I don't need to. I know he's right.

As we climb back into Tallulah, Jed says, "You know, if you're not comfortable telling me what happened at the party ..."

"I am," I insist. I'm not really, but something tells me I have to. I have to tell the truth, to the one person I feel comfortable telling it to. "Let's go somewhere, though. I don't want to tell you at home. In case you get, like, really aggro and yell and Dad hears you. Because if he knows what happened, he will literally kill Viggo."

"I might literally kill Viggo," Jed says. He gives a grim smile. "Or I might help you work out some other way to punish him."

"How could we possibly punish Viggo MacDuff?" I moan. "He's already got everything he wanted. He got perfect grades so he's going to be off to the best university. And, probably, by now he's got some other minion to do his bidding. Hell, he's probably taken up with Kacey Kuusela. She was always hanging off his every word. I used to think he wouldn't go for her because she's ... not really intellectual. But if he could change me he could change her. And she already has the fashion expertise. Plus, she's pretty ..."

I flinch at a memory of Viggo telling me I *could* be *almost* pretty "when I made a bit of effort".

At the time, I'd taken the scrap of a compliment, holding it in my heart like a warm comfort. "Almost pretty" was good, right?

And he'd given me constructive criticism for how I could improve myself. That meant he cared.

"You are very pretty," Jed says. "And beautiful. And cute. And … sexy." His voice croaks on the last word. He covers his embarrassment by continuing quickly. "And smart and wise and funny and … everything. You're everything, Connie-girl. To me, you're everything."

"I was never enough for Viggo," I say. Jed has moved closer. I can smell him. He doesn't smell like fancy aftershave like Viggo does.

He smells like Jed.

It's better.

"You are enough," Jed says. "Just as you are. Except …" he presses a finger to my forehead, "for that little voice in your head that says you aren't. That voice has to go."

I take his finger from my forehead and press it to my lips. He brushes the finger across my cheek, so slowly, so softly.

And then he leans in.

And it's nothing like my kisses with Viggo. It's not businesslike. It's not brief and to the point. It's gentle and lingering and so very comfortable. So right.

"Well, this is unexpected."

I break away from Jed. Leaning over to peer in Tallulah's window, a wry smirk on her tired-looking face, is Em.

"Em! Oh my Ben …" I squeak. "What are you even *doing* here?"

"Watching you and Jeremy make out," she says, laughing. "Which is not at all the vision I had when I thought of coming back to Tassie to rescue you."

"Rescue me? I—"

I realise I still have my arms around Jed's neck. I give him a brief smile—one that I hope says "we'll continue this later"—and remove my arms, wrapping them around Em instead. "You came home from your holiday early for me?"

She nods into my hair "I thought when you didn't return my calls that something was really wrong. I was worried. And plus, I have information. About Viggo MacDuff."

"We're not talking about Viggo MacDuff," I say, choosing to forget that Jed and I *will* be talking about Viggo soon. Or, at least, we would have been if Em hadn't shown up.

"Oh, I think you're going to want to hear this. See, I think I told you I ran into someone in Queensland. At a party, for my cousin's birthday?"

"Who?" I ask. "Not Viggo?"

"No," a voice says from behind Em. "Me."

I crane my neck. "Kacey?"

"I'm here too, by the way," says Patience, waving at Kacey's side. "Em and Kacey came over to ask where you were and, at first I wouldn't tell them because I knew you were on a romantic date with Jed, but then they told me what they knew and … Sorry, sis, I just had to. Because you're going to want to hear this."

FIFTY-ONE

I lift a shoulder. "And?"

"Didn't you hear me?" Kacey asks. "I said Viggo kissed me!"

"I heard."

Her perfectly plucked eyebrows shoot upwards. "You knew?"

"I didn't know. But I'd been thinking it was a possibility. You obviously thought he was the bee's knees. I thought you might try it."

Kacey shakes her head furiously. "Me? No. No way! *I* didn't try it. *He* tried it. I never liked him, Connie. Not like that. I mean, I thought he was hot when he first started at school … and yeah, I thought he was smart and … well, I wouldn't mind if some of that rubbed off on me. But I would never have tried anything with him. He had a girlfriend—you. And I like you. I'd give anything to be friends with you."

Now I *am* shocked. "Are you serious?"

"Why wouldn't I be? We've been hanging out lately, right? And I mean, I know we've never been exactly friends before but how could we have been? You and Jed were always a party of two

—and I *know* you called us the überclones—and then you were hanging off Viggo like a puppy dog. I thought that was a bit weird because I never picked you as a girl who'd go all doormat. But I figured you saw something in Viggo that I didn't. I thought he must treat you nicer in private than he did in public."

"He never did," Patience snaps.

"Why were you always so flirty with him?" I ask. "If you didn't like him?"

Kacey looks at her fingernails. They're painted bright pink, with palm trees and pineapples alternating on each finger. "I didn't mean to be," she says quietly. "I don't think I know any other way to be with boys."

"Oh, come on!" Patience cries. "Enough of all the deep-and-meaningfuls! Tell Connie what you told Em, Kacey! Tell her what you told me."

"When I turned Viggo down, he got kind of angry," Kacey says. "He kind of ... yelled at me. Called me worthless, stupid, ugly ..."

"Holy crap." My hand is pressed to my mouth. "He didn't ... hurt you?"

Kacey looks up at me, eyes shining. "Not physically. But ... a couple of the Landcare people walked in while he was going off at me. It was just before a meeting, see, and they came in and ... he stopped. Stopped yelling. But I noticed his hands were all tight. In fists. Like he *might* have hit me if the others hadn't arrived. Or, at least, like he wanted to."

"Why didn't you tell me?"

Kacey shrugs, her chin trembling. "I wanted to. But I didn't want to hurt you. And I thought ... maybe it's a one-off. Maybe you two had a fight, or he was stressed about something ... I wanted to give him the benefit of the doubt because ... well, he's Viggo MacDuff. Everyone looks up to him. And, plus, I liked you, so I wanted to believe he was actually a good boyfriend to you ..."

"But …" Patience gestures with her hand for Kacey to keep going. "Go on! Go on. Tell her the rest. Tell her about the video."

FIFTY-TWO

We sit together in the park where Jed and I used to play as children, and we talk about revenge.

There's Jed, Kacey Kuusela, Em, my little sister and there's me. We sit on the swings and on the rocking cars opposite, and we drink corner shop slurpies, and we talk about all of the ways we could destroy Viggo MacDuff.

There's a video.

After Viggo tried it on with her, Kacey confided in the über-clones. They convinced her that it couldn't be a one-off. They convinced her that she had to look into Viggo's history and find a way to make him pay. I think Jed and I underestimate the intelligence of the überclones. Either that or they'd watched *John Tucker Must Die* one too many times.

Anyway, Kacey did start investigating. And it turns out she might have a career in front of her as an academic researcher, because she dug up all sorts of dirt on Viggo.

Although the fact that she's a whiz at Facebook definitely helped, and that might not be quite such an asset in the world of academia.

But what she found out is this: there have been other girls like me. Girls plucked from obscurity and changed to fit a mould made by Viggo MacDuff. Girls he charmed and then discarded when they began to annoy him.

The first one was four years ago. He'd been at this for a while. None of them had lasted as long as I did, though.

A couple of the girls … he hurt. Like he hurt me. One of them caught the incident on video and posted it on YouTube.

The girl threatened to tell everyone who the guy in the video is. You only see his back, but if you've spent hours studying his back as he walked in front of you, you'll have no problem identifying him.

That's why he and his family left Sydney. The "study tour to Europe" was only a front. The MacDuffs did go to Europe for a few months, until the furore died down. And then, when they came back to Australia, they moved to sleepy little Bangarra. Where they thought Viggo's past couldn't catch up with him. Trouble is, Viggo's a leopard whose spots are welded on. His past became his present.

"He hurt another girl, didn't he?" Em says sombrely. "He hurt you."

"Don't try and deny it!" cries Patience. "I saw your ribs."

"I think it's time you told us the last memory," says Jed. "Then we can work out how we're going to take this guy down. Once and for all."

And so I tell them.

FIFTY-THREE

Memory 25

I tell them how Viggo arrived at my party, at nine, when the party started at seven. He gave me no apology, and told me straight up that he could only stay half an hour. He had "other commitments" that night.

I tell them how he didn't bring me a card, or a present. I tell them how he wasn't in costume, even though it was meant to be a pirate party.

I tell them how, when my dad came to shake his hand (something I now know would have been a strain for him, considering how much he hated Viggo), Viggo rolled his eyes and shook it as if he was under extreme duress.

I tell them how he refused to play the party games Jed organised, calling them juvenile.

How he kept checking his watch.

How he asked me to turn the music down.

How he told me—three times—that he'd have to leave soon as he had "important things" to do.

How he drummed his fingernails on the arm of his chair, and sighed and clicked his tongue.

How, finally, I got sick of it.

"Come with me," I said.

I grabbed him by the elbow and marched him off into the next room. Everyone watched. Everyone knew I was pissed off. Everyone knew Viggo was going to get it, big time.

Several people gave me the thumbs-up.

Not Jed, though. Jed called out, "Wait, Connie-girl. Your favourite song's about to start, on the mix-tape."

"I'll be back, Jeremy," I snapped.

I remember that now.

And I remember the hurt in his eyes.

But, at the time, all I could think about was Viggo. And my anger.

I don't know what it was. Maybe it was just the fact that I was dressed as a tough pirate queen. Maybe it was just that a year of being repressed was finally getting to me.

Maybe it was that Viggo really was being a Class A douchebucket and he needed to be called out on it.

Maybe I was a little bit drunk on the two birthday beers Dad had bought me.

Whatever the case, I was fired up.

"What in the Actual Hell?" I cried, not caring if Viggo thought I was blaspheming or being uncouth.

"What the hell me?" Viggo snapped, his voice low and cold. "What the hell you, Constance? You humiliated me! Dragging me out of there like that as if I was ... lesser than you. As if you had control over me. As if I was some ... servant. Some plaything. Don't you know who I am, you worthless piece of shit?"

I jolted. Viggo never swore. He never talked like that. And his face ... he looked so furious. So out of control.

Viggo MacDuff was never out of control.

I'd planned on saying more—calling him out for all of his rudeness that night, and for not buying me a present or dressing up or making any effort whatsoever. But now I'd forgotten how to speak. My lips were glued shut. I was terrified.

Viggo stepped towards me. "You useless, pathetic creature," he growled.

"How dare you attempt to humiliate me like that? How dare you attempt to bring me down in the eyes of my colleagues? How dare you presume you are important enough to do that? You are nothing. Nobody likes you. You are friendless. You are worthless."

"J-Jed," I whispered.

"What?" Viggo's cold eyes locked on mine.

"Jed is my friend," I whispered, trembling.

"Ha! Not likely, the way you've been treating him," Viggo snarled. "You've barely spoken to him in a year. You've lost him, 'Connie-girl'. And ..." A corner of his lip twitched into a twisted smile. "After what you just did in there, you've lost me too. You're completely alone now, Constance."

He was at the door by the time I could get my feet to work. I ran after him, standing between him and the door. Tears were streaming down my face. "Please, no!" I begged. "Please, Viggo. Please! Don't do this." I grabbed at his shirt. He brushed me away as if I was a mosquito.

"Get off me," he hissed.

"Viggo!" I grasped at him again.

"Get off me!"

Viggo pushed me, hard, in the shoulders. I sprawled to the floor. My heart was pounding.

Then, as I struggled to get up, he kicked me in the ribs.

"Pathetic," he spat as I lay there, aching and cowering, curled in a ball on the floor. "It's over. You've messed up big time, Constance. It's over."

The front door slammed.

I sat there for a moment, shaking.

I could hear the sounds of the party going on in the next room. I could hear laughing, cheering, squealing, singing.

Happiness.

I could hear it but it felt as if there was much more than a wall between it and me.

How could I ever feel happy again? Viggo was gone, and it was all my fault.

I dragged myself to my feet, wiped the tears from my eyes and went up to my room. I knew the people at the party wouldn't come looking for me. They'd be giving me and Viggo "space", not knowing that Viggo was taking all the space he needed—away from me.

Beezus was waiting for me on my bed. I scooped him into my arms and sat with him, rocking backwards and forwards, until I felt okay enough again to go downstairs.

I checked myself in the mirror on the way past. I looked all right. Face a bit pale, eyes a bit puffy, but nobody would notice anything was wrong with me. Not if they didn't really know me. Which nobody downstairs really did, apart from Mum and Dad, and they were having "grown-up time" watching crime shows on iView in the kitchen. And Patience knew me, of course, but she was playing Trivial Pursuit with the two school friends she'd been allowed to invite to my party.

And Jed, of course.

Jed would know.

Jed always, instinctively, knew my mood. Even though we hadn't been as close in the past year as we had for the rest of our friendship, I was still sure he'd sense that something was wrong.

And, maybe, part of me wanted him to sense it. Maybe part of me wanted someone to know that I was upset and ask me what's the matter. Maybe I wanted to tell someone what had happened.

No, that wasn't true. I didn't want to tell just anyone what had happened.

I wanted to tell Jed.

But when I got back to the party, Jed was gone. So were a couple of other people.

"They went back to Jed's house for a Star Wars marathon." The girl from the American Civil War group—the sandwich girl—said this with a smirk and taunting eyes. Then she turned away.

"That's fine," I said, to nobody in particular, as I settled on the couch by myself. But it wasn't. In previous years there was no way Jed would

leave my party without saying goodbye, especially not to have a Star Wars session without me.

Not even my favourite Ben Folds song starting on the mix-tape Jed had made for me could cheer me up.

Instead, it made me feel even more miserable.

"I don't get many things right the first time. In fact, I am told that a lot. Now I know all the wrong turns, the stumbles and falls brought me here."

"Here," I muttered, fighting back a fresh wave of tears. "Alone."

After the song finished, Jed's voice boomed out of the CD player. "That one was for you, Connie-girl. From me. Because it's how I feel."

"Yeah, you feel like I'm a loser, just like Viggo does," I whispered.

I knew the rest of the song went on to say happier things, things about being the luckiest person in the world because you got to be with the person you loved. But I knew that wasn't the bit Jed meant.

Like everyone else, he thought I was pathetic. He thought I was stupid. He hated me. He had to. That's why he left.

"No," Jed says, and I'm suddenly aware that my face is coated in tears, and I see his is as well. I've seen Jed cry before—he does it when he's listening to music, and he sobbed like a baby when Amy Pond was killed by the Weeping Angels in *Doctor Who*—but I've never seen the look of utter anguish that's on his face now. "No," he says again. "I left because I realised that night that I couldn't take it anymore. I couldn't take you loving him anymore."

"I'm sorry," I say.

"Stop saying you're sorry!"

When I look at Kacey, I see she's furious.

"Jesus. That fricking guy! That's how he does it. He makes you feel like you're nothing, like you're worthless, like you're always stuffing up and having to apologise for everything you do. He makes you feel like that so he can control you! Connie, I loved helping you choose all those outfits ... at first. I loved it because I enjoyed, like, getting to know you, but even I could see after a while that those clothes weren't right for you. It wasn't good for you to wear them. I even tried to tell Viggo. Remember I asked him to come and talk to me that day about 'Landcare stuff'. Yeah, I didn't really. I wanted to talk to him about how I was worried about you. He didn't want to hear it. He didn't care. He just tried to make a pass at me instead.

"Guys like Viggo don't care about us. They don't care about anybody but themselves. They don't care if they hurt you because you mean nothing to them. They just break you down and throw you away and leave you still feeling broken. It's bullshit. It's everything the feminists fought against. It's what we should still be fighting against."

I can't help laughing. Kacey Kuusela the feminist? Life really is full of surprises. "I think I underestimated you," I admit.

"I know." Kacey lifts her chin and smiles. "People do. I'm an überclone. We're shallow and vapid. But we're not how you think. Jane is an epic cook—she wants to be on *Masterchef*. And Karen wants to play violin in the national orchestra. And I— well, yes, I do want to be a fashion designer, but I'm also passionate about the environment. I know everyone thinks I only joined Landcare because of the boys, but I didn't. I want to create an environmentally friendly fashion line, using only sustainable fabrics, and contributing profits back into environmental causes. That's my dream. What's yours?" She raises an eyebrow.

I look at my Snoopy Vans.

Because I don't know what my dream is, now I'm not with Viggo. Viggo had my future all mapped out for me.

Without him …

"She can be anything she wants to be." My head whips around to look at Patience. "My sister is awesome," she says, smiling. "She's a brilliant musician, and an incredible artist, and you should read her stories! Oh my gosh, she could be the next JK Rowling if she wanted to be."

"Or the next Neil Gaiman or Marjane Satrapi," Jed adds, mentioning the names of two graphic novelists I love. "You should see her comics."

"I haven't worked on my comics for a year," I admit.

"Time to start again," Jed says firmly.

"Maybe you could write a graphic novel about all of this," Em says. "About Viggo MacDuff."

"Maybe you could write a graphic novel about it and get it published and *take him down*," Kacey says, smacking a fist into her hand.

"We have to take him down somehow," says Patience.

Everyone goes quiet. I know they're thinking about my story —my final memory of Viggo MacDuff. I look over at Jed. His face is less stricken now. More determined.

"I want to kill him," he says. He takes my hand and squeezes it.

"I want to kill him harder," says Em.

"I want to totally humiliate him and then kill him," says Kacey.

"Let's figure out how we're going to do it," says Patience.

While the three of them talk revenge, I lean my head on Jed's shoulder. I let him kiss my hair. I enjoy the feeling of rightness.

We're not together. Maybe we will be. I think we will be.

In time. I need time. Possibly space also. How very *Doctor Who*.

I listen to birds singing love songs to each other in the tree branches above us. I watch a lizard lying lazily in the sun. I look at the sunlight dancing on the water of the pond, the way it glimmers like it's been kissed by fairies.

"What if I just want to forget him?" I say to Jed. "What if I just want to go back to how things were before?"

"You can't go back," he says. "Viggo MacDuff changed you. You can't pretend none of it happened."

"I know," I say quietly. "I'm worried he'll always be inside me."

"Whenever you feel like that, you talk to me," he says. "I'll always listen. We can exorcise Viggo MacDuff together." He ruffles my hair. "I love you, Connie-girl. I always have. And I know it'll take you a while to get over Viggo, but I'll be here. I'll always be here. And—" His face turns serious, "if you want to go to the police … Connie, you probably *should* go to the police."

I nod.

I know he's right. And I know I should take action about what Viggo did. I've made a start. I've documented the bruises. I've written down my version of what happened. And I've told people.

It's a start. The next step will take courage. I think I have it in me. I hope I do. In the meantime, I'm going to let my friends have some fun.

I tune into the girls' conversation in time to hear Kacey say, "We could project the film on the wall at the graduation ceremony! When he goes to pick up his award!"

I smile. I know the revenge against Viggo is in good hands. I'm happy to watch it from the sidelines, for now. And I'll get my own back on Viggo MacDuff in another way, too. By finally finding out who the real Connie is.

I reckon I'll let Jed help me find it, but I know he won't want to define it. I know he'll let me discover it all by myself.

"You know what I want to do?" I ask, cutting in on the conversation.

"What?" asks Kacey.

"Can we go back to my house?" I ask.

"Sure," says Em, rubbing her hands together. "We can collect evidence to use in Project *Destroy Viggo*."

But I have another idea. Something I want to do first.

And so, in the back garden of my house, we all—with the addition of a cuddly Beezus and my bemused parents—watch as the advent calendar goes up in flames. And I feel like the twenty-five memories of Viggo MacDuff burn with it, turning to ashes and floating away.

I've kept a copy, of course, of the bits I might need as evidence. But the rest? That can burn.

I know that what happened will always stay inside me. That's okay. I don't want to forget, because I know remembering will make me stronger, but I want to stop making it important—making *him* important.

He's not important.

He's someone who came into my life, shifted things around and then left. And the girl I've become is different from the one who met him that day in the school hallway. But that's okay. She's better. She knows what she wants now.

Once the fire has died down, Jed takes my hand again. "So, what do you want to do next?" he asks.

"We're planning revenge!" Kacey cries.

My dad looks at her curiously. "Who are you?" he asks.

"Kacey Kuusela," she says, sticking her hand out. "Future sustainable fashion designer and head of Project *Destroy Viggo*."

Dad looks impressed. "Now that is a project I can heartily endorse. Let me know if I can help in any way."

"I'll help you too," I say. "Whatever information you need, you've got it. If you need photographic evidence of my injuries, you've got that too. And my memories. But do you mind if I leave you all now? I actually do want to start working on my graphic novel again. I'm itching to."

"Cool. But we'll talk more, right?" Em squeezes my shoulder.

I nod. "We'll talk more."

"And I'm so taking you into town shopping tomorrow," Kacey

adds. "For *Connie* clothes. The others might have been elegant—I do have impeccable taste—but they're not *you*."

"Oh, and we have to go to the Bangarra mall," Em adds. "You know that show you like? The one with time travel and the guy with the bow-tie?"

"Doctor Who?" I ask, sneaking a wry look at Jed.

"Yeah," Em nods. "Well, as I walked through it today with my brother, he got all excited because there was, like, this blue phone box set up in the middle of it. He kept saying, *Tardy! Tardy!* He's mental ..."

I can't speak. I just stare at Jed. *The likelihood of me and Jed getting together is about equal to finding the Tardis in the middle of the Bangarra mall ...*

"It is its own universe," he says, shrugging.

The others leave. "How did you—" I begin.

He holds a finger to my lips. "I didn't do anything," he says. "It's just timey-wimey magic. Trust me. I'm the doctor." Jed laughs and touches me on the cheek, so gently. "See you tomorrow, my new companion?" he asks.

I nod. "We'll go on adventures."

He winks at me and disappears.

In my room, with Beezus on my lap, I open a packet of Cheezels. I eat them, one by one, off my fingers.

Then, I pull out my sketchbook and a graphic novel marker and I draw a girl with cropped blue hair (with a fringe), and Vans and a band tee-shirt. I give her a cape, too, and a mask over her eyes.

She's a superhero.

Now I just need to work out what her powers will be. I know she'll have a sidekick—a ferret called Beezus. I know she'll fight against evil guys like Viggo MacDuff.

And there may be a storyline in which Daleks appear in Tasmania and start attacking people at Salamanca market and are taken down by my superhero, her ferret sidekick and an army of Ewoks who've joined forces with a pack of mutant Tasmanian Devils.

But the rest?

I start drawing. It's coming together.

I'll make it up as I go along.

ABOUT THE AUTHOR

Kate Gordon grew up in a very booky house, with two librarian parents, in a small town by the sea in Tasmania. In 2009 she won a Varuna fellowship, which led to publication of four titles with Allen and Unwin and Random House Australia. Kate was the recipient of 2011 and 2012 Arts Tasmania Assistance to Individuals grants, which means she can now spend more time doing what she loves. She was the recipient of the 2016 IBBY Ena Noel Award. In 2018, realising a life-long dream, she will have her first two picture books published.